# My Fair Assassin

## by C.J. Anaya

This is a work of fiction. Names, characters, places and incidents are either the product of the author's imagination or used fictitiously, and any resemblance to actual persons, living or dead, business establishments, events or locales is entirely coincidental.

Chapter One

Having someone tell you they've come to end your pathetic existence is probably an uncommon occurrence. I can't imagine that anyone intent on murder would have the decency to pause long enough to look their victim in the eye, state their mission and purpose, and with very little feeling explain that the end result of their victim's death will benefit an entire race.

Then again, what do I know?

There's always the slim chance that plenty of killers are far more civil seconds before committing such a depraved act, but how would any of us ever be privy to those morbid details when the victims never live to share said details?

I knew I'd never live long enough to share mine.

The well-muscled warrior standing several feet in front of me had made that abundantly clear. I studied him intently, deciding it would be best to memorize every inch of him in case I managed to escape and succeeded in describing my would-be assassin to the local authorities.

Right!

My need to drink in his image had absolutely nothing to do with his six-foot frame, broad shoulders, sharp, chiseled features, and flawless, crystal-blue orbs framed by a sturdy brow.

Insert wistful sigh here. And wasn't that the antithesis of what I should have been feeling?

Weren't murderers supposed to be ugly, unkempt psychos? This guy was a carbon copy of most of the Abercrombie models I lived to drool over. He had an otherworldly look and feel to him, and his clothing appeared to be made out of some kind of forest-green leather. His hands were gloved up to his knuckles, and his skin let off a golden, florescent glow.

I might have attributed his all-too-perfect tan to the San Diego weather, but I doubted other men in the vicinity were capable of making their skin glow a light golden hue whenever the sun's rays kissed them. I didn't think someone as imposing as this guy would have spent time throwing gold body glitter all over himself, but I couldn't figure out what else he'd done to get his skin to glimmer like that. He looked like a warm summer evening and smelled like the earth after a spring rain.

His hair was shoulder-length, shiny, and lightning white. Not the kind of graying white you might find on your local senior citizen, but the kind that looks like heaven.

His movements as he studied me and my dingy apartment were stiff and watchful. His expression was that of guarded curiosity, and when my cat, Nala, made a small whining noise from my bedroom down the hall, his stance came to attention and his arm muscles went taut as he withdrew a small dagger from a sheath at his waist.

Honestly, where had this guy come from, and why weren't we dating?

Oh, yeah. He was here to kill me.

"It's just my cat," I said, raising my hands in a placating

3

gesture. "My roommate, Jami, is out of town for the weekend."

"What?" He lowered his dagger and stared me down.

I didn't feel threatened by his gaze. I almost felt drawn to it, and I wondered if he was as curious about me as I was about him.

*Stupid! I am so stupid.*

Any other recently emancipated seventeen-year-old would have run screaming around her apartment in an attempt to get her worthless, noisy neighbors to call the cops, or at the very least, to come to her aid.

Not me, apparently. Oh, no. I was content to stare at the gorgeous criminal before me with all thoughts of fight or flight escaping my slow-witted mental processes. It was a little strange that he was more interested in killing me than kissing me. I don't say that to insinuate that I'm the most desirable woman in the world, but usually whenever I make eye-contact with a man, their pupils tend to dilate, they get this weird obsessive look in their eyes, and suddenly I've added an unwanted admirer and eventual stalker to my list of unwanted admirers and stalkers.

Truly, I didn't do it on purpose. It simply happened and I had no idea how to stop it. But this guy...he looked at me with the kind of indifference I'd been praying for from most men...and it totally bothered me.

Which was ridiculous.

"That noise you just heard was my cat. She's not much of a threat to you unless you're violently allergic to cat hair. So once you're finished...how did you put it? ...'regretfully ending my poor, pathetic human existence,' I'd appreciate it if you'd dump some cat food in a bowl on your way out." I folded my arms over my chest as he silently continued to take me in. "Just thinkin' out loud here," I added self-consciously.

4

This whole situation merely added insult to the injury that had recently become my life.

It was a darn shame, too. I'd only just discovered this morning that my ballet teacher thought I would be ready to audition for the San Diego Ballet Company in two weeks. I'd be eighteen by then and wanted so badly to dance professionally I did nothing but eat, sleep, and dream ballet. After sacrificing for so many years to pay for my own tuition—seriously expensive as I got older and the training became more intense—I was ready for this opportunity. I was also broke, having paid for this months tuition with my rent money when I lost my job.

Yet another reason why this murderous man's arrival felt like an added twist of the knife. I'd become emancipated and escaped my crummy foster home and my sleazy foster father, I'd landed a great secretarial position at a law firm which helped to pay the bills, and I was on the fast track to becoming a prima-ballerina. Things had finally been going right for me until I lost my job, couldn't pay my rent, and some delusional guy in a Peter Pan outfit had decided to come kill me.

So unfair.

"You face your imminent demise with honor and dignity." He nodded in approval, but his expression held a hint of confusion. "I must admit, I was not expecting such a brave display from one the likes of you."

"One the likes of…what is that supposed to mean?"

His eyebrows rose at my caustic tone.

Hey, I wasn't a fan of being insulted—or murdered either, but I was more practiced at defending myself against degrading comments than attempts on my life.

"You are human, and as we all know, humans are a cowardly, passive-aggressive race despite their propensity for devious and destructive behavior."

5

I placed my hands on my hips, feeling outraged.

"May I remind you that you are human too, and murdering me doesn't bode well for your own personal code of ethics? You're not exactly the poster child for stellar human behavior."

The handsome murderer shook his head in amusement.

"I am neither human nor a poster child. I have never heard of that race, to be completely honest with you." He took a step closer and gave me another searching look. "I would also like to clarify the circumstances surrounding your death. This is not a murder."

The audacity!

"You *are* human, albeit a crazy and deranged one, and you just divulged your plan to kill me. According to the laws of this land, that's murder." I met his challenging step with one of my own.

He gave me a wicked smile and took another step forward, no doubt trying to intimidate me.

"I'm not human. I'm a member of the Fae, and the laws of *my* land state that an assassination is not classified as murder when it is done for the good of the Fae kingdom and its ruling monarch. Also, I informed you of your impending death, and I'm giving you a moment to make peace with it before I send you on to the next phase of your journey." It was obvious he thought his actions were perfectly sound and reasonable. "I have kept to the strict code of honor all assassins swear to uphold in these circumstances."

Not only did I match his intimidating step forward with one of my own, but I followed through with my crazy impulse to laugh in his face.

"The Fae? As in faeries? Please! Assassin's code of honor? Look, I'm all for rationalizing bad behavior. I'm guilty of shoplifting occasionally while telling myself it's either break the law or starve to death, but at some point a line must be drawn. How about we draw that line at murder and avoid blaming our actions on creatures who don't exist?"

"You don't believe me? Do I look like a human to you?" He seemed angry at the thought.

It was then that I realized logic would be useless in this situation. My assassin was a few peanuts short of a plantation.

"You are completely off your rocker," I stated in a matter-of-fact tone.

His features took on a puzzled look, and I threw my hands in the air, totally exasperated.

"You know, I could stand here while you waste time monologuing about your crazy delusions of a different race and ask you how an obscure girl living in foster care for most of her life could ever be considered a threat to your mythical kingdom and its mythical monarch, but I'd much rather get this whole business over with." I rubbed my forehead and let out a harsh laugh. "Your timing is impeccable, considering my recent thoughts of throwing in the towel."

I sensed him take that last step forward, bridging the gap between our bodies, and suddenly I was staring at the tight lines of his chest through the strange fabric of his tunic. He surprised me by reaching for a strand of hair at my temple and rubbing it between his thumb and forefinger. It felt quite nice, and I had to bite my lip to repress the soft sigh that nearly escaped.

"I'm not sure I understand what throwing a towel around has to do with this conversation." He sounded a bit distracted. I looked up to find him reaching for more of my hair. He gently pulled some extra strands from my messy ponytail and began running all five of his fingers through them.

"It's an expression." I closed my eyes at the amazing sensations his fingers evoked. "It means I feel like giving up. I'm tired of fighting." Thick tears gathered at the corners of my eyes, and I fiercely blinked them into submission.

I thought I heard him mutter the words, *white roots*, under his breath, but couldn't be sure. It was an odd thing to say and made me feel nervous. He stopped playing with my hair and looked at me.

"You're a warrior, then? I must admit, I wasn't sure how you might be a threat to our reigning king, but perhaps your fighting skills have something to do with it."

He gave my hair a brief reprieve and stared at my ears. At least, I think he was staring at my ears. Then again, I'd felt terribly self-conscious about their shape for most of my life, and even though I saved up for some plastic surgery and had them fixed a while back, I sometimes forgot the mutated ends were no longer visible.

*Idiot. Get over your insecurities. He isn't staring at your ears. And seriously, why should you care.*

I shivered. "No, I'm not a warrior. I'm tired of starving all the time. I'm tired of fighting for food and shelter. I'm tired of getting fired every time a boss or coworker makes an unwelcome pass at me, which is exactly what happened a few days ago."

My would-be assassin gave me a bemused look and went back to playing with my hair, something I found terribly distracting. I pulled the thin strands out of his fingers and walked over to the small, square table leaning against the wall to my left. I grabbed an envelope, turned back, and waved it in his face.

"Do you know what this is?"

"I'm assuming it's some form of human

communication."

"It's a sweet little eviction notice my roomie left for me before she went on vacation because I can't provide for myself. I can't earn money fast enough to pay for my share of the stupid rent. My only other option for survival is something I would never in a million years contemplate, and so I'm left with no money, no food, no family, and this crappy 'I'm-kicking-you-out' notice."

"You have no family?" He reached for my hair again, but I stepped away before he could grab it.

"Foster care! Didn't you catch that? My parents died in a car wreck when I was a baby, and I have no other living relatives who can care for me."

"So you do not know how to fight?" He went for my hair yet again, but I was too preoccupied with the date on the eviction notice to defend myself against his relentless onslaught.

If I didn't come up with six hundred dollars by the end of the week, I would be out on the streets again, digging in local, restaurant garbage cans for food and fighting old, homeless ladies with stolen grocery carts for a bed at a run-down women's shelter.

"No, I don't know how to fight, but I *will* be destitute by the end of the week."

That thought was more than depressing—it was devastating. I'd searched long and hard to find a roommate willing to take me on despite my age and total lack of income. Then I'd landed that sweet secretarial position at JP Morgan & Ross even though I only had a GED and zero experience. I met Jami at the grocery store within the same week, and it just so happened she needed a roommate fast. It had all panned out so well six months ago, and look how quickly it had fallen apart.

Thank goodness Jami wasn't here to witness my

demise. With any luck, this handsome assassin would kill me quickly and dispose of my body without anyone being the wiser. I threw my eviction notice on the floor and finally had the presence of mind to stop him from mauling my hair.

"Would you quit that and just end me already? The suspense is killing me."

I might have laughed at my unintentional pun, but something crazy happened. The moment my hand touched his, a small electrical current skipped through my fingertips and created a faint glow between our hands.

I gazed at the eerie luminescence in surprise and lifted my head to find him staring at me with a mixture of disbelief and uncertainty etched across his features.

"That was...unexpected. I wasn't aware humans possessed supernatural tendencies."

"We don't. I'm just as surprised as you are."

I might have attributed the strange light to hallucinations as a result of food and sleep deprivation, but my assassin was witnessing it too. Maybe *he* was a hallucination. I was having an imaginary conversation with an imaginary hot guy who was here to kill me with his imaginary dagger.

He pulled his hand away and stared at it, looking extremely perplexed. Then he reached out for mine again, lacing his fingers through my shaking ones. The glow from the contact of our skin burned a little brighter this time.

He held our entwined fingers up to his eye level, lifting my five-foot-five frame to its tippy-toes.

"I've never seen anything like this in a human before. I've studied everything there is to know about your race, and not once did my studies cover this type of physical phenomenon."

"You're human, so why on earth would you feel the need to study them?"

He lifted his gaze from our hands to my eyes and held it there.

"I will state once again that I am Fae and an assassin of the highest order. Any seasoned assassin knows he must study his mark to effectively kill it. You must know all of your enemy's strengths and weaknesses in order to prepare for the unpredictable circumstances inherent in my profession."

I felt a slight chill tickle my spinal column at the casual way he discussed death. This Looney Tune may have been handsome, but he was also deadly. Encouraging him to talk about his delusions was probably better than having him act out any of them.

"Wow. That's quite the field of study. Do you kill anything besides humans?"

"Of course. Any criminal who is a threat to the Fae is swiftly dispatched by the Fae's assassins. The majority of these criminals are vampires and werewolves. Humans are rarely targeted for assassination, though it has been known to happen. I was most eager to receive this assignment due to the rarity of the mission. I've never actually seen a live human before today."

I looked at our linked hands and the glow our body heat produced, and for some reason I felt wholly content. I'd always been a very restless individual. I never knew when I'd be moving or when the next assault on my person would take place, with all the various foster fathers and brothers. I couldn't remember a single moment in my life when I had ever felt truly safe, and yet standing here with this human-who-supposedly-wasn't-human, I felt more protected and serene than I cared to admit. I wasn't even bothered that he was here to assassinate me. At least

11

he was being civil about it.

I was totally losing it!

This guy was here to kill me, and I was holding hands with him? How about a moving rendition of *Kumbaya* while we were at it?

I tried pulling my hand out of his, but he had a much stronger grip on my fingers than I'd realized.

"What's wrong?" he asked, refusing to release me.

"Hello! You've come to kill me! Do you always get this friendly with your victims?"

He pulled me in closer and dipped his head down toward my neck, inhaling deeply and then straightening.

"Interesting," he muttered under his breath.

"What?"

"You have a very distinct woodsy smell. I'm not completely certain killing you is advisable at this point."

"My woodsy smell is now the deal breaker in all this?"

He gave me a serious nod. "Of course. Your smell is extremely significant."

"Well, how *extremely* bizarre! Does that mean I can have my hand back?" I tried again to free my tingling fingers from his grasp to no avail.

He watched me struggle, amusement creasing the faint smile lines around his kissable mouth.

"You are not what I was led to believe. I fail to see how you could be a threat to my race when you can't even extricate yourself from my weak hold on your hand."

I rolled my eyes. "I think it's great that you're having second thoughts about murdering me. That's progress, really it is, but if you're not going to kill me, how about figuring out a way to pay my rent so I don't find myself homeless again?"

"Consider it done."

"I'm sorry. What?"

12

His eyes lit up at the ideas I could almost envision formulating within that beautiful cranium of his.

"I need to learn more about you before I report back to my superiors. They will want to know why I aborted this assignment. I think it best to live here with you for the time being until I come to understand how the monarchy could have made such an egregious error concerning your welfare."

I struggled to wrap my brain around this new development.

My assassin was now my roomie?

"Live here? You can't live here. I already have a roommate."

"Don't worry about that. I'm sure I can convince her to find another place to dwell."

"I have a cat."

"I am not, as you said, violently allergic to cat hair."

"I have self-respect!"

"I don't see what that has to do with anything."

I tried throwing my hands up in frustration, but only succeeded in throwing one of them since I had not been able to free my other hand from its current prison. Not that I was putting up too much of a fight, and seriously, who could blame me, right?

"You were ready to assassinate me fifteen minutes ago, and now you expect me to let you live here while I lie awake at night, wondering if you're going to change your mind and kill me in my sleep?"

He brought my hand to his nose and inhaled deeply. I raised my eyebrows at this disturbing behavior.

"Has anyone ever commented on your serious lack of social skills?"

"Killing you is out of the question. The thought will never cross my mind again, but someone wants you dead, and I must find out the reason for this. The assassin's code is very clear about protecting the frail and defenseless."

"I am neither frail nor defenseless. I've negotiated the murky waters of foster care for years and come out on top. I can take care of myself."

"I am your caretaker now. Until I understand what games are being played here, you are under my protection. There is something very strange about all of this."

"It's funny that *you* should be the one to acknowledge that, Mr. Crazy Pants."

The corner of his mouth lifted slightly. "Crazy pants? I'm not sure I understand your meaning. I am not wearing this thing called 'pants,' and clothing lacks the necessary intelligence required for insanity to exist."

I looked heavenward, hoping I would find patience for this handsome assassin's strange inability to understand English.

"It's slang. You're not supposed to take it literally."

His eyebrows drew into an adorable V. "How else is the English language supposed to be taken? Do humans never mean what they say?"

"That annoying behavior tends to happen more when we're dating."

"Dating? What is dating?"

"What is...seriously, you don't know what dating is? Were you born under a rock?"

"No, a fir tree, but that's a very personal question to ask, and we hardly know each other."

I stared at him for a few seconds and half-heartedly pulled on my hand.

"Why do you keep trying to pull away from me?" he asked.

"You're holding my hand."

"Yes, I am your protector now."

"Does that mean you'll be holding my hand for the rest of my life?"

He contemplated my question seriously.

"No, I imagine that would be inconvenient for both of us, but at the moment, our contact makes my skin tingle and heat in a most pleasant and surprising way. Do you not feel it?"

"Oh, I feel it."

"Then why do you want me to let you go?"

"Does the phrase 'personal space' mean anything to you?"

"No."

"All righty, then."

I sighed heavily, though secretly I couldn't help but love the feel of his hand in mine or the fact that he acknowledged the strange chemistry between us. Talk about Stockholm Syndrome!

"Let's get back to the part where you mentioned paying my rent and moving in."

His face brightened at this and then he motioned to the sofa next to us, quirking an inquisitive eyebrow at me.

"Do you mind if I sit down for a moment?"

"I...suppose that's fine."

He immediately moved to the couch and made himself at home. Unfortunately, he still had hold of my hand and refused to relinquish it so I went right down with him. I decided not to complain since *he'd* decided not to kill me. I wasn't about to thank him for it though. The way I saw it, the right to live wasn't something I needed to ask permission for.

He held tightly to me as if he was afraid to lose the luminescence from our contact. His beautiful eyes rose to mine and then we just sat there facing each other.

15

Cozy.

I couldn't figure out if I was having a nightmare or some blissful fantasy because there was no way I wasn't dreaming this entire thing.

"I can use my powers of persuasion to convince your roommate to find another place to live when she shows up again."

"Powers of persuasion, huh? Good luck with that," I muttered.

He didn't seem to notice my incredulity since he continued discussing his plans like they were destined to come to fruition.

"I will happily pay for your accommodations, and in return you will allow me to live here with you so I can investigate this unorthodox situation. And since you appear to be nothing more than a frail, weak, non-threatening individual, I shall offer you my protection should the need arise."

"Thank you...?"

He appeared pleased at my response and rubbed a finger against the top of my hand, creating sparks of golden light as he did so. I stared again at the magical glow and then shook my head, trying to restore order to the crazy churning of my thoughts.

*Wake up. Wake up.*

"Wake up," I shouted.

"I am awake," he said in some surprise.

I startled at his voice and opened my eyes.

"I am, however, extremely tired and wouldn't mind a few hours of sleep. I would be most grateful if you showed me to our room."

My eyes bugged out of their sockets.

No way in hell was I sharing a room with a dude who'd originally planned on killing me. I didn't care how sinfully kissable his lips looked. If he was up for a catnap, then I was sooooo taking advantage of that and getting myself and Nala outta here. I'd be a fool not to, even though the temptation to stay and drool over him as he slept might have briefly crossed my thoughts.

Briefly, okay.

I hadn't completely succumbed to my assassin's otherworldly good looks...yet.

"Our room? There are two rooms in this apartment. You can sleep in Jami's room as long as you don't mind being ensconced in bright, pink satin."

The discontent on his face made me wonder if he might go for his dagger.

"I cannot protect you if we are dwelling in separate living quarters."

"The rooms are right across the hall from one another. You could literally launch that very pointy dagger of yours from one room to the next and maim any perceived threats to my person without any problems. I promise."

He mulled that one over for a moment and then shook his head. It was interesting to watch the emotions play across his face as he went from one thought to the next. The tightening of the muscles in his jaw-line signified his dissatisfaction with my response, and damned if that didn't make him look even more appealing.

"I'm afraid your suggestion is unacceptable. Until I understand why the monarchy considers you a threat, you will remain with me."

"As your hostage?"

His lips quirked in amusement.

"Of course not. You're not a prisoner."

I shook my head, ripped my hand from his—to which he let out an outraged grunt—and rose to my feet, grabbing my purse from the coffee table and throwing it over my shoulder. This dream was over. I hoped the reality of my unemployment and the need to find a new job would snap me out of this crazed hallucination I was trapped in. With any luck, my assassin would evaporate due to the monotony of filling out applications for McDonald's and Burger King. I turned toward the door and ran smack dab into his muscular chest.

Sigh.

He placed his hands on my shoulders to steady me.

"What are you doing?"

I took a step back to remove the alluring warmth and weight of his hands upon me. My teenage hormones couldn't handle the contact.

"You may be paying the rent, but I still need money for food, clothing, tuition, and other necessary girlie things. I figure if I'm not a prisoner, then I'm free to go out and get a new job."

"That's completely unnecessary. I will provide for your needs."

I'd been waiting for years for someone to say that to me; for someone to give me the green light, simply stop surviving, and enjoy my childhood...or what was left of it, but the way he said it—like his word was law and there was nothing left to discuss—made me revert to an I-am-woman-hear-me-roar mentality.

"Are you planning on killing me?"

"No."

"Are you planning on keeping me locked up in my room for the next decade?"

"Of course not."

"Are you going to provide me with tampons when my next period hits?"

His face balked at that. "I'm afraid I have no idea what tampons are, but I'm familiar with a human female's

18

menstrual cycle. The similarities between our females and yours are nearly identical in that department, and no, I do not wish to overstep my bounds."

His idea of overstepping was hell and gone from mine.

"Then I need to go get a job."

"Not without me."

I glared at him, but he looked annoyingly unaffected by it. I stepped forward, deciding I should take charge of my hallucination and just walk through him. With arms locked at my sides, I rammed right into him. He didn't budge an inch while the impact nearly launched me flat on my butt. His quick arm around my waist saved my very bony arse from some painful bruises.

"Was that some strange human custom I failed to uncover during my studies?"

My face burned with embarrassment—seriously, who lets a hallucination embarrass them—as I adjusted my purse, pushed out of his wholly unwelcome embrace, and moved toward the door like the independent woman I'd become.

Ha!

Chapter Two

"Do you normally avoid eye contact with the male species?"

My assassin's pointed question brought my startled gaze up to his.

"What?"

He turned and pointed to the Burger King establishment we had just left.

"When you asked the pimply, prepubescent male for an application, you did so with your eyes on the counter. Then when the manager came out to talk with you about your availability, you kept your eyes at chest level." He grabbed my arm and pulled me closer to him as a few teenagers with skateboards nearly rolled right into me. "Strange custom," he muttered as we continued walking. His gaze followed the young skateboarders with a bewildered expression and then his eyes returned to mine. "However, when one of the young ladies working there greeted you with a smile, you did not suffer the same problem."

Dang. This dude was observant. That did not bode well for any possible escape attempt.

"I've found over the years that anything male will

generally react to me with a strange kind of fixation that borders on obsessiveness. I'm not tooting my own horn here, either. It just happens. I'm not much of a looker, but eye contact is always the first step toward gaining another longtime stalker."

My assassin's face scrunched up in confusion.

"Tooting your own horn? I don't see what playing an instrument has to do with whether or not men notice you. I would also like to know what exactly a 'looker' is, and I'm hoping there is no relevance between the word looker and hooker."

I tried not to choke on a laugh as I removed myself from his grip.

"You can't take language so literally. Sometimes words and phrases don't make sense if you do."

I kicked a small stone in my path and studied my ancient tennis shoes. My toes were practically bursting through the worn material. I figured they still had a few more months of wear and tear, and then it would be back to The Salvation Army for more used shoes. Couldn't complain, really. Not when services like that were available, but every once in a while I dreamed of being ridiculously frivolous and buying brand name shoes that probably wouldn't last me a month before they wore out.

"So if you *are* intent on staying here for a few days in order to protect me from…whatever…I think you'd better tell me your name. Unless, of course, you'd rather be referred to as, *Hey, You.*" I snorted at my own joke and kicked another loose stone before me. After the silence extended for another awkward beat, I glanced up at my assassin who pondered my request with a level of seriousness that seemed a bit excessive.

"C'mon. I never did catch your name," I prodded.

"That's because my name isn't something I'm capable

21

of throwing at you."

Face palm.

"No...what is your name?"

He haughtily lifted his chin and squared his shoulders. Was his name so awful he had to prepare himself?

"While I'm sure, *Hey, You* is a nice enough name in the English language, I would prefer another title entirely."

"Okaaay. Wait, what do you mean title?"

"Since you are my charge, you may call me Master."

I shook my head in disbelief. Every conversation with this guy was a lesson in narcissism.

"Pass."

"Pass what?"

"It'll be a cold day in hell before I start calling you Master."

His cheeks puffed out as he blustered a response.

"But that's impossible. Hell will never endure the blessing of a soothing winter's breeze."

"Exactly."

His eyes narrowed as he finally understood my meaning. Once again those delicious muscles in his jaw tightened, making me salivate just a little.

"If you are not amenable to this moniker, you may address me as Guardian."

"No."

"Protector."

"Nope."

"Your Majesty."

"Seriously? Did your parents never name you?"

He stopped rather suddenly, and I turned around to face him. His ire at my question was unmistakable.

"Addressing me by my given name is considered a distinguished honor, one you are most certainly unworthy of. No human is."

I rolled my eyes at this self-aggrandizement and continued walking. Either he was delusional or I had gone absolutely crazy. Neither scenario sat well with me.

"Fine. From now on I will refer to you as Chuck."

He caught up with me in two easy strides.

"Why would you do that?"

"Because it strips away a bit of that unbearable pride you wear like a shield around you and helps to convince me you're really not that intimidating."

"I don't like it."

"I don't care."

"You haven't given me *your* name."

My eyebrows narrowed. "You don't know the name of the person you were sent to assassinate?"

"I don't need to know the name. I am given a scan of your biological signature which allows me to find you no matter where you are or what dimension you exist within."

My heart sank at this. I'd assumed that running away was an option, but if this guy really was a member of a mythical race and what he said was true, then I would never be able to hide from him for long.

Then again...I studied his muscled physique as he strode proudly next to me, appearing slightly mesmerized with his surroundings, but not in a way that actually allowed him to relax a little.

I supposed I could suffer through his presence indefinitely.

"Are you going to tell me what your name is then?" he asked.

"Fair is fair. You give me your real name, and I'll consider telling you mine." I gave him a teasing smile, hoping it might loosen up that stoic facade of his.

The assassin I had just officially dubbed Chuck opened

his mouth to let out what was most likely another complaint, but I caught something out of the corner of my eye that caused me to grasp his arm and roughly pull him forward.

"We need to keep walking, and not in the direction of my apartment," I said in response to his startled grunt.

"What is the matter?"

I dared a glance behind me and stifled a frustrated moan. I'd suffered several stalkers in my day, foster fathers included, but none of my stalkers had ever been as persistent or as freaky as Eddie Lima, a man who was once my manager at a fancy Mexican restaurant called Tasty Tijuana's just one year ago. His unsavory connections with a Mexican gang in the LA area had made him a very dangerous man to say no to...but I'd said it anyway on several occasions. He was partly the reason I'd pushed for emancipation. I literally couldn't hide from the guy if I was stuck in the same foster house until I became an adult, and there was no way my foster parents were going to help protect me. They didn't give a hoot about what happened to me.

How in the world had he managed to find me?

I saw Chuck peek a glance over his shoulder, turning back to me with a puzzled look.

"You wish to avoid this man?"

"Yes."

"But I believe he wants to speak with you."

"He'll have to take a number."

"Sometimes I wonder if you're speaking English."

I quickened my steps as we crossed an intersection. I didn't think breaking into a run was a good idea since I didn't know if Eddie had come alone or if he had a few of his gang buddies with him. Entering a crowded store or eating establishment and waiting it out was probably going to be our best bet. I really had no idea what Chuck was capable of when it came to defending himself, but other than the dagger he flashed earlier that day, I didn't see any other weapons on him. A gun would make short work of Chuck, assassin or no assassin, and I found myself worrying about that—worrying about him!

This was a screwed up situation.

I glanced behind me again only to see Eddie closing in with a maniacal look in his eye. The guy was seriously scary.

"Chuck, we need to get into a more crowded area as fast as possible. I'm sure Eddie has a few of his friends closing in, and he won't take a chance that he might lose me again."

"My name is not Chuck. I take it this man is not your friend?"

"No. He's obsessed with me. He thinks I belong to him and refuses to leave me alone."

He grabbed my arm and hurried me faster as his long legs took even longer strides.

"He wants you for his wife?" he ground out.

"More like a trophy. Once he kidnaps me, he probably won't ever let me go. I'm not interested in being chained inside a room and raped for the rest of my life."

Chuck's features darkened as he pulled me into a run. Instead of running toward the shopping center at the end of the block, he took a left and headed toward an abandoned area in the back where large trucks dropped off shipments for the shopping center's fast food and store establishments.

"You're going to box us in. Eddie will have brought reinforcements, and we won't be able to take them all at once." He threw me behind him and turned around to face the approaching threat.

"You insult me with your low opinion of my ability to protect you. These pitiful, overly tatooed humans are no match for a member of the Fae, especially one such as me."

We were doomed.

I rubbed my temples in slow circles as I heard heavy footsteps approach. I looked up and nearly swallowed my tongue in fear as Eddie and three other thugs walked straight toward us. Every single one of them carried a hand gun.

"You steppin' out on me, Crysta?" Eddie lifted his chin and glared at me.

"Crysta," my assassin muttered with some surprise. "Now that's interesting."

Since four guns were currently trained on us, I decided not to ask him what in the world that was supposed to mean.

"Cheating on you requires that I actually be in a relationship with you, Eddie. You and I both know that's never happened."

His face turned stormy, but I didn't care. I fully intended to go out with a bang.

"I made it clear how I felt about you, Crysta, and then you disappeared on me. Most people would consider my interest in them an honor."

I was about to make another snide retort that would most likely get Chuck and me killed when my assassin lifted his hand, palm forward toward our assembled executioners, and muttered something unintelligible.

"What are you doing?" I whispered.

Eddie and his men let out jeering laughs.

"As long as Crysta is under my care, you'll not lay a hand on her." Chuck had both hands lifted now, and he continued with his gibberish as our aggressors mocked him.

Eddie took a menacing step forward.

"Is this your bodyguard? Why would you pick a dude so puny?"

Puny? Were we looking at the same assassin?

"I've had enough of this," he continued. "Fill this hombre with lead and bring me the girl."

Bullets flew the minute the order left his lips, but they never made it to their intended target. Instead, the bullets hit some invisible wall a few feet from Chuck.

My eyes widened and my jaw hit the floor.

"Shoot him," Eddie screamed.

His minions continued to fire shot after shot while I watched in amazement as each bullet pinged into some unseen force and dropped to the ground.

This was crazy. For the first time since meeting Chuck, I began to wonder if maybe I *wasn't* having some super vivid hallucination. He was here, he was real, and he had just put up some bullet-resistant force field with a few muttered words and some hand signals. Eddie and his cronies could attest to that, not that I'd ever consider them reliable witnesses, but they were witnesses nonetheless.

Chuck pounced the minute they emptied all of their bullets. I really don't know how else to describe it. He moved as gracefully as a deadly panther, weaving in and around each thug as he brought them to their knees with one swift jab here, a kick there, and even a few stabs with his dagger. Within seconds, Eddie's cohorts were on the ground completely unconscious. I hoped they were unconscious anyway. Murder was not on my bucket list.

I'd been so engrossed in the lithe movements of my assassin that I failed to see Eddie sneak up behind me before it was too late. He wrapped an arm around my waist and pulled me against his chest, bringing his gun to my temple.

He hadn't fired a single shot. He'd let everyone else do the shooting.

Chuck took a step forward. His nostrils flared, and the tightening of his jaw could have decimated granite.

"Let her go," he said. His voice was so calm and tranquil it actually scared the hell out of me. Eddie must have been ready to pee his pants.

"Not a chance, esse." He turned and spoke into my ear. His fetid breath making me want to gag in revulsion. "Don't you dare try to freeze me out like last time. I've got a gun to your head, chica, and I'll use it the minute you try any of those freaky tricks of yours."

I cringed at the reference he made to some of my not-so-normal abilities in front of my assassin. I wanted it kept a secret for when I made my escape, though I guess it hardly mattered now since Eddie was the one holding me captive at the moment.

Eddie turned his attention back to Chuck. "I'm leaving alive, and if you know what's good for you, you'll let her leave with me."

"Separatum," Chuck said as he lifted his hand and swung his arm wide. I felt an invisible force push me forward as Eddie released me and fell back. My assassin flicked his wrist, sending something jetting through the air. I heard a loud thunk and spun around as Eddie hit the ground with a dagger buried in his chest.

I opened my mouth to let out a scream, but nothing happened. My vocal chords were paralyzed. Instead, I dropped next to Eddie's body and grasped his hand when he let out a wheezing sound and gave me a pleading look.

"We've got to get him to a hospital," I screeched, finally finding my voice.

"He attacked you. He intended to harm you, and you

want to save his life?" Chuck's tone seemed a bit detached from the situation. Heartless, even. A cold-hearted assassin through and through.

"I know that, but that doesn't mean I can just sit back and let him suffer and die like this. It's murder."

"It's self-defense."

I glanced up at him with a lone tear burning its way down my cheek. I took in his puzzled expression and then the shock that spread across his face as he registered my devastation. He knelt down next to me and placed a hand on my shoulder.

"Crysta," Eddie wheezed. He squeezed my hand to get my attention. "I just wanted to keep you. I don't...know why...what came over me...just obsessed with you. You were always so...kind to...everyone."

"It's not his fault," Chuck said with some awe.

My gaze shifted sharply to his.

"What do you mean it isn't his fault?"

"Without a glamour, you are impossible to resist."

"What?"

Bewildered, I let go of Eddie's hand as Chuck pushed me aside and pulled his dagger out of my old manager's chest. Eddie let out a scream that brought more tears to my eyes. Chuck placed both hands on the man's chest, muttered a few words, and moved back as the wound quickly healed.

"How?" I brought my gaze back to Chuck's face. The look in his eye was difficult to interpret. It was as if he was seeing me for the first time. Maybe that's not quite the right way to put it. Like he was recognizing me. It was surreal to say the least.

"My name is Jareth," my assassin said as he extended his hand and grabbed mine.

I was too confused, scared, and, let's be honest,

suffering from some serious shock to come up with a response to that. I mean, he was introducing himself now? Random.

He pulled me to my feet, wrapped an arm around my shoulder, and directed me back the way we had come.

"What about Eddie and his guys?"

"They'll be fine when they wake up. Most importantly, they won't remember you ever existed."

I let that sink in as I allowed myself to lean into the steady and reassuring warmth of his embrace.

"You...you saved me."

Chuck...no wait...Jareth gave me a small smile, one that barely turned the corners of his lips.

"I saved you." He pressed his lips to my forehead, kissing me with a tenderness I had never experienced before.

Anyone would have been sobbing hysterically due to the violence I'd just witnessed, but I had seen so many horrible things in my short life that I had become quite desensitized to the horrors that plagued people who looked like easy targets. People like me. I'd suffered all sorts of terrifying situations without batting an eyelash, but one moment of kindness from Jareth completely undermined my ability to keep my cool.

I bawled like a baby all the way back to my apartment while Jareth held me close and whispered comforting reassurances over and over again.

Chapter Three

"So your name is Jareth?" I asked.

My assassin sat on the couch next to me with one hand entwined in mine, looking afraid to let go in case I burst into a paroxysm of wailing and snot-crying after he'd finally managed to help me calm down. I probably looked hideous with my red nose and puffy eyes.

I'm an ugly crier. It can't be helped.

My question caused the corners of his lips to turn up in a barely perceptible smile. At least, I hoped that's what it was. Maybe he had changed his mind about assassinating me and figured the best way to end the hysterics was to kill me and be done with it.

"Yes, and your name is Crysta."

I blinked, remembering his initial reaction to my name.

"You thought my name was interesting. How so?"

He remained silent for a moment and then shrugged his shoulders saying, "It is an uncommon name amongst my people."

"I assume that goes without saying. I doubt most human names ever end up being used by a race who thinks so lowly of us."

Not that I was any closer to buying into this whole Fae

31

thing. I'd had just enough time to talk myself out of whatever had really happened back there with Eddie and throw myself behind my pitiful shield of denial.

"I am not so certain that humanity is what we're dealing with when it comes to you?"

"What is that supposed to mean?"

"I cannot go into detail on my suspicions at present. I will simply have to continue to observe you and your daily routine in order to find out what is really going on here and why the monarchy could ever find someone like you a true threat."

I narrowed my eyes at him and shifted on the couch in order to get a little more distance between us...which did absolutely no good. His vice-like grip on my hand was sending me a very clear message.

*Resistance is futile, earthling.*

"I'm not entirely comfortable with the idea of being analyzed and examined for the unforeseeable future, and you still haven't explained to me what you did back there." He furrowed his brows as if he didn't know what I was talking about. "Hello! You blocked bullets, healed stab wounds, and wiped memories with a wave of your hand and a few muttered words of gibberish!"

"Latin."

"Excuse me?"

"Well, some of it was in Latin. The rest was a mixture of Celtic and Gaelic idioms. The Fae have mastered many human languages over the years, but Gaelic is one I truly prefer."

I raised my eyebrows. "I'll make a note of that for future reference. Now would you please tell me how the heck you managed to do all of that? It was like magic."

He shook his head in amusement. "Why are you asking for an explanation when you just gave yourself the answer?"

"Magic doesn't exist."

"You understand exactly what you just witnessed, yet you frown at me and deny everything your eyes have shown you." He leaned over and moved a wavy tendril of hair from my forehead. "Do you remain in denial due to the improbability of my own gifts or are you really in denial about yours?"

"I don't know what you're getting at."

He leaned back into the couch cushion and studied me for a moment. I didn't like the heat that stole over my face.

"You are lying. Even Eddie mentioned something about freezing him out."

"Also a slang term. Freezing a person out means you remove them from your life. You do everything you can to exclude them from all of your activities." I held my breath, hoping he would buy the BS I'd just handed him.

His look was speculative as he said, "I suppose I'll have to study the use of slang terms during my extended stay with you."

"Look, I am very grateful for the way you defended me against Eddie and his lackeys back there, but I think we need to reevaluate our living arrangements. You really can't stay in the same apartment as me."

"Don't you find it interesting that every male you encounter becomes strangely fascinated with you almost as if their power to resist you or even think rationally when confronted with your presence is non-existent?"

His departure from a subject I thought important to discuss managed to disorient me a little. I couldn't think of anything to say other than the obvious.

"Well, you certainly don't seem to have any problems resisting me. You're the first man I've met who hasn't wanted to claim me for himself."

"Haven't I?"

His heated look sent a strange burst of fire through my tummy and down my thighs. I could have sworn the blue of his eyes took on an otherworldly glow for just a second, but as I looked deeper within their depths the glow faded and his eyes resumed their natural color.

I wasn't sure what I had been getting at or where we had left off in the conversation so I decided to start all over again.

"Okay, well...it's nice to know your name is Jareth instead of Master. I'd offer to shake hands with you, but we've kind of jumped past that formality." I squeezed his hand with the one he had yet to abandon. He smiled and squeezed back. Then I sat staring at him like an idiot while the warmth from his fingers slowly blossomed up through my arm and straight to my heart.

I let out a soft gasp at the same time he did. Jareth studied our entwined hands, no doubt looking for some kind of explanation for our strange electrical reaction to one another.

That's what I planned on calling it, anyway. Just a strange electrical reaction.

This was crazy. I couldn't have him living with me, studying my every move, and giving me strange jolts every time we touched. Not that there would be any touching after this. In fact, there was absolutely no reason to continue holding his hand.

I unraveled my fingers from his and rested them on my lap. He didn't look happy with my actions, but at this point I didn't care. I had an assassin sitting on my couch who just so happened to wield magic, and now he thought he was my roommate.

I'd had better days.

My stomach made a loud gurgling sound.

"Are you hungry?" He quirked an eyebrow at me in amusement.

I felt my face grow warm with the force of his half smile.

His full smile would most likely knock me off my feet.

"Yes, I'm hungry. Getting shot at does that to me. I'm just going to grab some food from the fridge." I stood up to go, but he grabbed my hand and stood with me.

"Why are you holding my hand again?"

"From now on, I'll need to maintain the appearance of your mate in public in order to discourage more unwanted interest from the opposite sex."

"Now you're pretending to be my boyfriend?"

"Mate. A much more binding and permanent commitment."

"If it's all a farce, then the terminology and level of commitment attached to either word doesn't really matter, does it?"

He glowered at my words as if I'd just insulted him again.

"But I'm only going to the kitchen."

His eyebrows narrowed in confusion. "The kitchen?" He said the word *kitchen* as if he were rolling the newness of the consonants and vowels around in his mouth. "Where is this...kitchen located?"

I threw a thumb over my shoulder. "Three steps that-a-way."

Swiveling toward my left, I pulled on his hand and led him into my kitchen, which looked more like a glorified walk-in closet. When it comes to the issue of shelter versus homelessness, however, beggars can't be choosers. As long as the apartment has a fridge and a microwave, I'm a happy camper.

I had simple needs, really.

"Will you let go of my hand, now? I don't think we're going to run into any persistent male suitors within this small cooking area."

He paused to look at me as if he didn't understand my meaning.

I tried a different argument. "All of this personal contact is a little strange, don't you think?"

He looked at our joined hands, deliberating for a moment before shaking his head and then adjusting his hand so his fingers interlaced with mine.

I sighed in annoyance and tried to forget how nice his hand felt in mine because it wasn't the kind of normal reaction a hostage was supposed to feel with her captor.

*And what a lovely captor he is.*

Not liking where my thoughts were taking me, I turned back to the fridge and pulled it open with my free hand. My face fell when I took in the pitiful contents of the stingy apparatus. Was it too much to ask for a magic cooler capable of producing your heart's most delectable food cravings out of thin air?

I reached for a bruised apple and took a quick bite, then remembering my manners said, "Would you like something to eat?"

Jareth smiled and grabbed my wrist, the one attached to the hand holding my juicy apple. Bringing the fruit to his lips, he took a bite right next to the space where my mouth had been. He maintained his intense eye-contact as he chewed slowly, swallowed, and then pulled my wrist close to his mouth again. Just when I thought he was going to... I don't know...kiss it...bite it possibly, he switched his trajectory and took another bite of the apple.

I swallowed hard and drew in a shaky breath.

"We *do* have other apples in the fridge."

He swallowed his last bite and pulled me closer.

"I like sharing with you."

He brought his lips an inch closer to mine where I felt his warm breath envelope my face. He smelled of summer leaves and recently trimmed grass.

"But I thought humans were beneath you."

"You're not human, Crysta."

"Of course I am."

My brain was screaming out a warning that distance from this guy was going to be the key to my survival, but his grasp on my hand and wrist and his constant need to breach my personal space were beginning to wear me down.

Kissing him was inevitable, and something I'd wanted to do since the moment he'd appeared in my living room uninvited.

Nala's loud meow broke the intense moment between us. I glanced down to see her wrapping herself around Jareth's leg.

Traitor. Or possibly my savior?

I quickly pulled myself from his grasp and went to the cupboard for some cat food. I didn't think Nala needed the food, but I definitely needed the space. I'd almost let a complete and total stranger kiss me when he'd originally been sent to kill me.

I needed mounds of therapy. Plain and simple.

"That was interesting," Jareth muttered under his breath.

I ignored him and grabbed Nala's bowl—which was already halfway full of food—pouring an unnecessary amount of cat kibble into it. I set it down and turned, fully intending to head to my room and lock myself in there for the remainder of the evening, but I balked when I realized that my tiny walk-in closet of a kitchen required that I squeeze past Jareth to attain my goal, and he smirked at me like he knew exactly what I was trying to do and wasn't about to make it easy for me.

I drew in a deep breath, preparing myself for the physical contact, and took a hesitant step forward.

"I think it's time for me to call it a night."

"Call what a night?"

I brought a tired hand to my forehead and vigorously scrubbed.

"Ah, hell's bells. I mean, it's time to hit the hay. Hibernate for the evening. Crash for the night. It means I'm ready for a good night's sleep after having an assassin break into my apartment and threaten to kill me, then threaten to protect me, then actually make good on said threat by conjuring up a force-field and stabbing a man in the chest, then healing the man and wiping his memory. I'm seriously hoping that when I wake up tomorrow morning, this will have all been a horribly deranged dream brought on by several years' worth of abuse, maltreatment, and homelessness."

Jareth was in front of me faster than I could blink, grabbing hold of my shoulders and forcing me to look at him, but not before I took note of the light created by the contact.

"Who abused and mistreated you? When were you homeless?"

His righteous wrath on my behalf left me staring at him with my mouth hanging open. I quickly shook my head, pulled away from his grasp, and maneuvered myself around his intimidating form, heading out of the kitchen and down the hall toward my bedroom.

He followed—of course—wrapping an arm around my waist and pulling me against his chest when we were halfway down the hall.

"Crysta, you have not answered my questions," he

ground out.

"And I never will. It won't do either one of us any good, and I have no desire to go into nauseating detail about all of the things my foster fathers and brothers tried to do to me over the years."

*Or what I managed to do to them in order to save myself.*

Yeah. I never intended to go into detail about that.

"I am not accustomed to such blunt refusals, Crysta. In my realm, when I ask a question, I expect to receive an answer." His arm tightened around me further, and his other arm encircled the front of my shoulders, locking me in place.

"Get used to disappointment, Jareth. You're in my realm now."

I shouldn't have done it. Honestly, it was the worst possible way to reveal how abnormal I was, but Jareth's overbearing manner and the events of the day had thoroughly pissed me off. I placed a hand on each of his arms and focused my energy through them, reaching for the cold, the frigid ice that always existed within me, that always threatened to push to the surface and completely take over my reason and control.

His arms stiffened and he grunted in surprise as dark crystals formed on his forearms. I ducked under the icy appendages and continued down the hall and into my room. Turning around to face my handiwork, I folded my arms and casually leaned against the door frame. His arms were completely encased in ice, held out before him as if he were cradling someone—like me—close to him. His look of absolute astonishment was more than perfect. It was priceless.

"I may appear weak, pitiful, and defenseless, but I have a few tricks up my sleeve."

To my surprise, a delighted grin slowly spread across

his face as his gaze moved from his frozen arms to my unconcerned stance. He winked at me. The arrogant assassin actually had the audacity to wink at me even though he was clearly the one at a disadvantage here. Then he closed his eyes and mumbled a few words under his breath. An orange heat spread from his chest to his arms, dissolving the crystal ice from his person, melting it into oblivion.

Well, crap! If it ever came to a real fight with this guy, my neat little parlor trick would give me maybe a two-second advantage. I'd revealed a highly bizarre ability and he hadn't even batted an eyelash. I was seriously considering tranquilizers at this point.

He bridged the distance between us in one easy stride, but I refused to move from my casual position against the door frame. I would not let this guy intimidate me. His smile led me to believe that he wholeheartedly approved of my behavior.

His behavior, on the other hand, had left me more than a little mystified.

"You're certainly full of surprises, Crysta, and you had every right to attack me the way you did. I will adhere to your wishes and refrain from forcing you to speak about unpleasant experiences, unless you wish to share them with me."

His proximity made my thoughts churn, forcing me to take in a deep breath, cursing the air that held his overpowering scent.

"I appreciate that," I said after a moment of uncertainty.

He placed a hand at my waist and drew me to him, apparently not finished with our conversation even though I was more than ready to be alone in a room with him...er...without him...definitely without him.

He touched his forehead against mine and breathed me

in for a moment. It was surprisingly intimate and calming all at the same time.

"Just know that I am happy to unburden you of all of your past fears and pains should you ever feel inclined to share them with me. You may not believe this, Crysta, but you can always count on me to provide for your every want and need."

"Even though I'm a freak," I whispered.

"I assume you are referring to one of your natural abilities; the one you used defensively. If that makes you a freak, then I suppose I am one as well. You are not the only person in this apartment capable of...freaky things."

I nearly giggled at his first use of slang and how unnatural it sounded as it left his mouth. Then it hit me. His acceptance. The way he'd looked at me with fondness and...well...a little bit of pride after I'd iced his arms in place. He hadn't been frightened or called me names. He accepted it because he was just like me in a way. Very different from most people.

"Thank you," I mumbled, forcing back the unwanted lump forming in my throat. I was not going to cry in front of this guy again. Feeling uncomfortable with this influx of emotion, I stepped out of his embrace and backed my way into the bedroom. As I tried to close the door I was met with resistance. I glanced up at him questioningly.

He looked almost apologetic. "As I stated earlier this morning, I will need to keep you in my line of sight."

I straightened my spine and glared at him.

Warm fuzzy moment over.

"You are not sharing a room with me."

The corners of his lips turned up at my stubborn refusal to acquiesce to his wishes.

"Then you will leave the door open so I can see you at all times."

So he was back to playing the role of overbearing tyrant, was he?

"What about privacy?"

"This word does not exist in my world."

"Don't give me that. You speak our language well enough to have come across the word privacy in your dictionary. I need to change into my pajamas, and you are not going to watch me do it."

"Your sense of modesty is an oddity to me, but I shall turn my back to you so you may change into something more comfortable."

"How terribly generous of you."

"Yes, it is."

"If you so much as quirk an eyebrow in my direction while I change, I'll freeze more than just your forearms."

His mouth twitched again before he nodded. "Understood." Then he turned around and faced the hallway.

I quickly flipped the light on and rummaged in my drawer for a comfy cotton shirt and some shorts, all the while keeping a close eye on Jareth's back and cursing myself when I allowed my eyes to rest a little too long on his nicely formed backside.

"Okay," I said as I walked to my bed. "You can turn around."

He turned and sucked in a breath when he took note of my clothing.

"I don't understand why you wanted me to turn around when you were wearing more before than you are now."

I crept under my covers, not liking the heated look he gave me.

"Please, just my legs are showing."

"It is enough to be truly distracting."

"I'll take that as a compliment."

He let out a heavy sigh and then sat himself down just inside the doorway.

"You're not going to sleep in Jami's bed?" I asked.

"As you stated earlier, warriors such as myself are not interested in ensconcing themselves in pink satin. A bit undignified."

I let out a hearty laugh as I snuggled under my covers.

"Hey, Chuck, would you turn the light off please?"

He let out an annoyed groan, mumbling something about being reduced to a simple house slave as he stood and flipped the light off and then sank back down to the floor again.

"My name is not Chuck, Crysta."

"I think it suits you."

"I think the next time you call me that there will be severe consequences."

"Oh, please. What are you gonna do? Give me a timeout?" I snickered at the thought.

"Since you seem to highly covet what you refer to as personal space, I'll simply grab you and kiss you for as long as I see fit."

I nearly choked.

"You're a terrible assassin, you know that?"

"How so?"

I tried to smother a laugh at the offense that laced his question.

"You came to kill me and now you've decided to protect me. You think you're the one in charge, but you've been willing to listen to me a time or two despite how arrogant and stubborn you are," I paused as he let out a snort, "and now you're threatening to kiss me. Assassin's Guide 101: You're not supposed to get emotionally involved with your victims, Jareth."

"Too late for that," he mumbled.

43

I shivered at the low timbre of his words and figured he was right. It really was too late for that.

At least it was too late for me, and that scared me to death.

I had to figure out how to get rid of this guy.

Tomorrow.

Chapter Four

"The sun is up, Crysta, and I've prepared a delicious breakfast for you."

I let out an undignified groan at the sound of Jareth's overly upbeat tone and turned to face the wall, pulling my pillow over my head. Not only was he still here and not a hallucination—though who knew, really—he was a super annoying morning person. The kind who oozes purpose and unrivaled determination. A real go-getter.

Yeah. I'm not usually *that* person until I've imbibed several ounces of caffeine. And even then, I generally fail to accomplish much. Plus, it was Saturday. I didn't have a job to go to and my ballet classes didn't start until Monday afternoon.

"Just because the sun is up doesn't mean it's time to *wake* up," I mumbled.

"That's exactly what it means. Unless people in this realm hibernate for certain periods of the day, and I don't remember that item being discussed during my studies."

He'd planted himself on my bed and was now leaning over me. I snuggled deeper under the covers to avoid him, but then he started tugging on my hair.

"What time is it?" I asked.

"The digital clock on your dresser reads five-thirty."

I moaned even louder this time.

"I'm not getting up at five-thirty in the morning just because you decided to hold me hostage in the middle of the summer."

"I don't understand."

"If it were the middle of the winter we wouldn't be having this conversation until a few hours later."

My warm cocoon was rudely breached when he suddenly ripped the covers away.

"We have quite a few things to accomplish over the next week, and the first item of business involves assessing your humanity."

"Come again?"

"We also need to discover how many abilities you have and how powerful each one is."

I curled into a tiny ball and squeezed my eyes shut.

"I don't have a plethora of abilities like you, Jareth. I just freeze things when I get emotional and that's about it. Not that I've ever talked about it with anyone or behaved as if freezing things is totally normal, but it's really not as amazing as you're building it up to be."

"Not yet, anyway. That's why teaching you to focus a little better is going to do wonders for your overall protection."

I rolled over to face him and lifted myself up on one elbow.

"You're going to teach me how to defend myself with my strange, uber freaky power?"

His eyebrows narrowed. "I feel like carrying a dictionary is an absolute must when I'm around you."

I hopped out of bed and headed for the bathroom. "Give me ten minutes to girl-ify myself and I'll be ready to party."

"Not English. That was definitely not English," he muttered.

I barricaded myself inside my bathroom and turned on the shower. Then I faced the mirror and winced at the dark circles under my eyes. I did a double wince at the white roots peeking out through my otherwise honey-colored hair.

That's right, folks. My hair had gone white long before I managed to take my first baby steps.

It had been one of the many reasons countless adoptions had fallen through the cracks. According to my various social workers, my unnatural looks and excessive fussiness made it impossible for any family to seriously consider me for adoption. My hair color was just the tip of the iceberg when it came to the complaints from my many foster families.

I'd spent hundreds of hours attempting to dye my hair the kind of hue normal teenagers had, but the color would only stay for about a week before it washed out completely, and I was back to looking like a prematurely-aged freak of nature. This week I'd dyed it blond for about the millionth time, and it looked as if I would need to go shopping for another box of hair color.

Soon.

I turned my back to my undesirable reflection, stripped, and then stepped into the heavy stream of steamy water, allowing its warmth and pressure to alleviate the tension in my neck and shoulders.

Within ten minutes I was out, scurrying to my room with a towel tightly wrapped around my figure, relieved to hear Jareth moving around in the kitchen. By the time I finished dressing in jeans and a white T-shirt, my new roomie was already tapping on the closed door.

His muffled voice sounded impatient. "I told you I had

47

breakfast ready, Crysta. It's going to be cold by the time you...um...girl-ify yourself. Whatever that means."

I opened the door and then crossed my arms over my chest. "There's hardly any food in this apartment. What in the world did you actually cook?"

"Why don't you walk down the hall and find out?" He gave me a mischievous grin and stepped back to let me pass.

Mystified at his behavior, I headed down the hall and then stopped dead in my tracks at the wide array of food spread out on the coffee table, entertainment center, and even different places on the floor. It was like IHOP had vomited its entire menu in my living room.

"First of all, I..." I cleared my throat and started again, "Where did you get all of this food, and how did you have time to prepare it?"

"Those are not really important details at the moment," he said from behind me.

I spun around at the unexpectedness of his proximity. I shouldn't have been so startled since he'd done nothing but invade my space since the moment he'd entered my life. I took a step back and placed both hands on my hips.

"What do you mean these details aren't important? When someone apparates an entire restaurant into my living room, I want to know exactly how it happened."

He smiled and nodded toward the food. "Pick out something to eat."

I gave him a frustrated sigh and turned around, narrowing in on one of the items I could actually eat without becoming physically ill. I carefully tip-toed around the various plates of pancakes, crêpes, and Belgian waffles until I arrived at the coffee table where a large bowl of strawberries sat.

I grabbed it and presented it to him like a student might

present a term paper to her teacher. "All right. I have my breakfast. You planning on eating the rest?"

He raised an eyebrow at my selection. "Very healthy, but not nearly enough to fuel your *human* body for the next few hours. Pick a second item to go with the fruit."

I placed the strawberries on the coffee table, bit the inside of my lip, and nervously cast my eyes about for something else. My various foster mothers and fathers had taken serious offense to my odd eating habits. The fact that their spaghetti and meatballs, steak and eggs, or chorizo and tortillas left me violently ill didn't seem to matter. I was simply an ungrateful whelp who refused the kindness and charity of those considerate enough to take me in, feed and clothe me, and provide an opportunity for my education. My palms started to sweat just thinking about it.

I saw another bowl filled with blueberries on the entertainment system and delicately stepped forward. I gingerly pulled it down and presented it to Jareth.

"There you are. Will two servings of fruit suffice?"

He raised yet another eyebrow, but this time a small smile hinted at the corners of his mouth.

"You've retrieved the fruit portion of your meal. Where's the protein?"

Feeling nauseated, more at his possible reaction to my response than the thought of consuming actual meat, I cast my eyes around the room and spotted a bowl full of pecans, cashews, and peanuts. Next to it was a plate that held what looked to be cubed tofu. I set the blueberries next to the strawberries on the coffee table and then made my way to the furthest corner of the room where I grabbed the nuts and tofu and made my way back to the table, feeling pleased that I hadn't had to offend him or explain my eating preferences.

This time his smile stood out more prominently. "No bacon? No sausage or chicken and waffles?" The questions came out a little too innocently.

I swallowed hard and shrugged. "I don't really like meat, and I don't enjoy breakfast foods made with processed white flour."

I moved around the table to sit on the couch, believing my response to be reasonable enough.

"Why?" he shot back.

Keeping my eyes lowered, I reached for the blueberries. "Fruits and veggies just taste better."

"What about eggs?"

"I've never developed a taste for them." My ears grew hot at his intense scrutiny.

"Interesting."

I sighed. "I wish you would stop saying that."

"Well, I think this little experiment was extremely informative."

He came to sit beside me and reached for the bowl of nuts, grabbing a few and throwing them into his mouth. I gave him a sidelong glance and took the bowl of nuts from his hand.

"This was an experiment?"

"Yes, to see if you eat like other humans. Obviously, you don't."

"I'm a vegan, for crying out loud. There are tons of vegans out there. Is that such a crime?"

"Vegan? Is that what humans call this type of diet?"

I shoved some berries in my mouth, recognizing that I was entirely too defensive and the next thing I said would probably include a few expletives.

"Because this is exactly the type of diet the Fae adhere to," he continued.

I choked on a berry and coughed it up while Jareth

patted me on the back. Recovering quickly, I turned to stare at him, wondering if he was making a joke at my expense.

"You mean...you don't think what I eat is weird? You aren't mad at me for not eating your ham and eggs or French toast and pancakes?"

He shook his head in wonder.

"Why on earth would I be mad at you for something like that?"

"I've had people call me ungrateful in the past... because I wouldn't eat the food they prepared for me."

"Wouldn't or couldn't?"

Geez. I'd never had anyone try to understand the reasoning behind my food choices, but I certainly didn't want to talk about all the reasons I was an unlovable foster child.

"Crysta, consider the whys behind your choices and habits. Don't you see it? You only eat fruits, nuts, specific grains, and vegetables."

"That's because I don't like the taste of anything else."

"That's because your body can't *process* anything else." He let that sink in for a moment before he said, "You're just like me."

I shook my head at the thought of me being just like anybody else when all of my life I had been an anomaly, a blight, a discolored stone amidst a backdrop of sparkling, precious gems.

Before I had a chance to respond to his outlandish claim, he stood up and grabbed another bowl of berries from the desk against the wall. Handing them to me he said, "Eat quickly, Crysta, we still have quite a bit more experimenting to do."

I stuffed another handful of berries in my mouth and slowly chewed as he smugly sauntered his way into my kitchen. I seriously wished he'd get bored and saunter his way out of my life.

I didn't want to know what other experiments he had planned for me, but if it involved unearthing more characteristics that substantiated my foster parents' claims of me being a freak of nature then I wanted nothing to do with them. I grabbed some nuts and a few strawberries and hurried down the hall. If I could get my purse and simply walk out of the apartment, maybe he wouldn't notice my absence for a few seconds. Long enough to get a minute or more to myself. If he got lonely, he could go bond with Nala. Plus, I really needed to go buy some more hair-dye. I'd be all white-haired by the end of the day if I didn't.

Acting as if I didn't have an insane, otherworldly stalker shuffling around in my kitchen, I retrieved my purse from my bedroom, returned to the living room, and stopped short at the sight that greeted me. Every single plate of food that had been scattered on the floor was gone.

"What the he—"

"Good. You're ready for our next little adventure," Jareth said, walking in from behind me. He folded his arms and took in my stunned expression. Then he turned and surveyed the room. "Did I not clean it to your liking?"

"Where did all of the food go?" I said.

"I sent it back."

"You sent it back. Back where?"

"Back to where it came from."

If it had been said by anyone else but Jareth, I would have assumed I was being mocked. I leaned against the wall and shook my head.

"So...you just conjured up the food out of thin air and

then sent it back into some supernatural breakfast void?"

He chuckled and gave me a look like, *Ah Crysta, you sorry, naive little human.*

"I sent the food back to some restaurant that claimed to serve everything you love about breakfast."

"Ha. I knew it was from IHOP."

"Well, shall we?" He offered me his arm, totally behaving as if making Belgian waffles and French crêpes appear and then disappear was as normal as taking out the trash in the morning.

Yeah. No matter what I'd seen Jareth do, I was still stubbornly refusing to believe that all of this was really happening to me. If it wasn't a hallucination then it was death, and paradise looked a lot like a handsome faerie named Jareth surrounded by several bowls of fruit.

I surrendered myself to the idea that I was both crazy and dead and took the arm he offered me.

"I suppose so. What new experiment are you interested in doing now?"

"I want to see how your skin reacts to certain temperatures."

I did *not* like the sound of that.

"You don't have to see anything. I can tell you exactly how my skin reacts to different temperatures."

He pulled me to the middle of the room and then wrapped his arms around me in a tight bear hug.

"You could tell me, but it's much better for me to know exactly what I'm dealing with here."

"What? Jareth, why do you have a death grip on me in the middle of the room?"

"Hold onto me tight."

He mumbled a few words under his breath and pulled me flush against him.

The floor beneath me tilted to the left while my stomach

took a nose dive to the bottom of my feet. The walls around us dissolved like a melting picture as the pressure within the room built to a suffocating crescendo. I squeezed my eyes tight and pressed myself closer to Jareth's chest.

A loud pop burst within my ears, causing the pressure to lessen and soon the floor beneath my feet felt solid again. Well, kind of solid. I opened my eyes only to discover my living room had disappeared. Where there should have been a dingy sofa, a hammock swung slowly between two palm trees. Instead of the bland, gray carpet I was used to, sand pressed between the toes of my sandaled feet.

"Where are we?" I whispered.

"Somewhere along the coastline of Santo Domingo. Here, you need to get out of the shade and into direct sunlight for this to work."

What he said barely registered as I fought to accept the idea that Jareth had somehow transported us to an entirely different location. How was it even possible? As he pulled my body out from under the shade of the palm trees my skin began to itch like crazy. My eyes shot to the sky and the severity of my situation finally dawned on me. I dug my heels into the sand and tugged on my arm as hard as I could.

"Stop, Jareth. I can't expose my skin to this type of weather."

He did stop, but he didn't allow me to move back into the shade. I felt the first blisters swelling on the backs of my hands.

"You were able to go out in the sun when we went to apply for jobs at those hamburger establishments."

I tugged more vigorously against his hold. My face was itchy and my toes were burning. "That's because the weather is fairly mild in San Diego and I usually have sunscreen on. I didn't get a chance to put any on this morning. My skin can't handle anything over 85 degrees unless I cover up."

I pulled harder, but he held on like a merciless pit bull, studying my skin with great interest. "It doesn't seem like your skin can't handle it."

*Just you wait.*

I tried to latch onto the icy core within me, but my panic had hit me so hard and fast that I couldn't focus. The blisters and burns forming would take a long time to heal, and it would be a painful process.

"You're barely in the sun. Just come out to the beach and get in the water for a minute. You'll feel much better." He pulled me along as I continued to fight for all I was worth. I let out a scream when the blister that had been forming on my hand burst and clear liquid leaked down my wrist.

Jareth turned at the sound of my distress and his eyes widened in horror. He quickly scooped me up and carried me back to the shade, but by that time it was too late. My entire face, arms, neck…anything that had been exposed was covered in blisters, and being held by him was absolute agony. I wouldn't be able to go out looking for work for at least three weeks. And what about my ballet classes? What about auditions for the company? I'd never be able to dance like this. Tears seeped down my face, making the burns and blisters sting even worse.

Jareth said a few rushed words in Latin and the air pressure built around us yet again. I didn't really register at what moment we made it back to the apartment. The minute he set me down, the blisters on my feet exploded, pain shot to my cranium, and everything around me went black.

Chapter Five

I expected heat to scorch my skin as I began to come to, but the warmth that surrounded me didn't bite at my nerve endings or irritate any of the open sores I knew to be covering my body. The feathery sensation of soft fingers running through my hair made my eyelids flutter as I fought to take in my situation.

"Crysta, I should have listened to you. Please wake up." Jareth's voice was tinged with worry and true remorse. "I didn't expect your reaction to be so severe. It's unprecedented, really. Most common folk don't blister and burn the way you do."

My eyes flew open and took in Jareth's concerned frown peering over my face. Then I realized he was cradling me in his lap. The heat from his skin giving me comfort rather than pain and misery.

"Of course they don't," I said, referring to his previous comment. "Most people can handle being in the sun even without sunscreen for longer than thirty seconds. I told you I was different. I already knew exactly what would happen, and you didn't listen to me."

His eyes darkened for a moment. I thought he was angry at my criticism until he leaned his head back and snuggled me closer to his chest, encouraging me to rest my head against him. I gingerly did so, still conscious of the blisters on my face and hands, but the contact gave me zero pain. I glanced at the backs of my hands resting in my lap.

No blisters. No burns. Nothing to indicate that my skin had virtually melted under the intense rays of the sun.

"I am unaccustomed to…listening to others or…taking direction from others unless those directions or orders come from my superiors. Generally, I'm the one giving orders. It is difficult for me to consider myself wrong or misguided when certain facts I have collected suggest otherwise. I am sorry, Crysta. You know your body better than I do, and I should have listened. I've sworn to protect you and instead I caused you severe injury and pain."

I lifted my head to look at him and saw that his remorse was genuine. The furrows between his brow and the sorrowful look upon his face made my anger with him dissipate immediately.

How does anyone stay angry in the face of such humble repentance?

"It's fine," I said, giving him a reassuring smile. "Now you know how my skin behaves in the extreme when it comes to certain levels of exposure to the sun. The only thing we need to clear up is what happened to all of the blisters? It usually takes me much longer to heal when I get burned."

"I healed you, and then I wrapped a protective charm around your person. You won't have any more problems with the sun while you remain in the human realm."

"Wait? You healed me? Permanently?" The rest of his sentence caught up with me. "What other realm would I possibly travel to?"

He chuckled and tucked my head back under his chin. "Yes, I healed you. Yes, the charm is permanent, and as far as other realms go, I don't think you're ready for that. You seem intent to deny what is so painfully obvious."

"What are you talking about?"

"There are many faeries in my kingdom who are sensitive to the sun like you are, but because they do not possess as strong of a connection to the seasonal element of winter, they are mostly unharmed. Their skin becomes irritated, but nothing like what happened to you generally occurs unless…"

"Unless what?" I was seriously intrigued by the notion that there were faeries out there who reacted to the sun the way I did.

"Unless their affinity to the seasonal elements—more specifically, winter—is so deeply rooted within them that the magic reacts catastrophically to its seasonal counterpart."

"I didn't comprehend any of that."

He gave me a pensive look. It was obvious he wanted to say more, share something more with me that might shed some light on the subject, but he was hesitant to do so.

"The Fae monarchy considers you a threat to their realm, but I grow exponentially concerned with each passing minute as to why. The more I understand your nature, the more I understand their motivation. Based on what I've learned thus far, I'm afraid this may not be the misunderstanding I had previously assumed it to be. You're still in very real danger, Crysta."

"And you're still not making any sense. You really think your king has a legitimate reason to fear someone like me? How threatening do I look to you?"

He studied me with a smile.

"At the moment, you look docile and sweet, but that

sharp tongue of yours could flay the thickest of hides. One should be wary."

"Right. When you return to your realm and discuss my demise with your king, be sure to put that on your report. The docile and sweet part, I mean."

He frowned. "I don't wish to return to my own realm... at least...not without you."

"Not exactly safe for me there. What with your king wanting me dead and all."

"I don't believe the order for your death came from him. He has many other things to oversee, and the Assassin's Order isn't one of them. His chancellor is head of that department."

"Well, it would seem his chancellor is missing a few key facts concerning my case. Like the fact that I'm a harmless teen who just wants to be left alone."

"I'll never let anyone hurt you. You have my solemn promise. Which leads me to our next order of business."

"And that is?"

"Self-defense. If you had more control over your powers, you might have fought me off a little better than you did on the beach. You lost focus and allowed panic and fear to overtake you."

I gave him a frosty glare, wishing it had the power to ice his attractive backside to the couch.

"Even if I *had* managed to access my...power...all I know how to do is freeze on contact, and you've already demonstrated how useless that tactic is."

He gently set me on the couch and then stood up, turning to face me.

"I want you to practice freezing me without contact."

Seriously, where did I even start?

He waited for a moment, but all I had to offer was a vacant stare. He shook his head impatiently and then bent down to eye-level, placing one hand just below my clavicle and above my heart. The heat from his hand spread a disconcerting warmth throughout my chest.

"Access your core as you usually do, but instead of keeping the power internal, you project it outward with your thoughts."

"How?"

"Your thoughts are essentially the steering wheel behind your power. You limit your range when you limit your thoughts, but if you visualize your power as an extension of yourself, you can build up enough pressure and intensity for your element to become an external force you can control."

"So, you want me to visualize frost shooting from my hands?"

His eyes lightened in approval.

"Precisely." He stood, stepped around the coffee table and turned again to face me. "Now, access your power, steer with your thoughts, and freeze me in place."

"What if I hurt you?"

He let out a comical snort and shook his head which totally pissed me off.

Fine. If he thought this first attempt was going to be that pitiful, he was seriously mistaken. I was going to ice the smirk right off his handsome face. I closed my eyes, reached for that frozen core—easy to do considering how irritated I felt—and visualized a frosty blast of air hitting him right in the face. I felt the power chill my insides as I brought it forth, and then ice shot from my hands in staccatoed bursts. I opened my eyes in disbelief, noticing the tips of my fingers tinged in blue, almost as if I had frostbite.

"That was amazing," I said. I finally looked at my handiwork when I heard Jareth let out a pitiful moan.

His eyes teared up and a faint redness crawled up his neck as he used both hands to cover his groin...which, incidentally, was also covered in ice.

"Was it your intent to deny me the privilege of siring children?" he asked through clenched teeth.

My eyes widened in surprise and then a burst of laughter escaped my lips.

"I wasn't aiming at your...at that particular...I was picturing your face." I fell back on the couch and let the giggles overtake me while Jareth glared at me. I wiped the mirth from my eyes, and tried to defend my actions. "I happen to be sitting down, Jareth, and that's where... maybe I should have stood up to do this. Then I would have shot you in the chest instead?" I howled with laughter as Jareth's glower became more pronounced.

"Indeed," he said with a grimace. He closed his eyes, whispered under his breath, and soon heat blossomed from his hands, melting away the residue of my frosty attack.

"Better?" I asked as he shook his legs out and walked the length of the room a few times.

"I suppose we can consider that first attempt a success despite your unfortunate lack of aim."

"I thought my aim was perfect."

"You would."

He gave me a smile that caused my heart to jolt within my chest. I ducked my head to avoid his clear gaze and saw that my fingers were back to their normal color.

"You were right, Chuck," I snickered to myself. "That particular maneuver would have come in handy at the beach."

"Did you just call me Chuck?"

I realized my mistake just as Jareth pulled me from the couch and into his arms.

"I believe I was very clear concerning the consequences of such an offense."

He inched his face closer to mine, his eyes flickering to my lips.

"I forgot," I said in a panic. I pushed against his chest, but it was like attempting to displace a concrete building. "I swear to you, I will never call you Chuck again."

"To be completely honest with you," he lifted my chin and placed a soft kiss just above the corner of my top lip. The resulting tingle made my knees shake. "I'm more than delighted that you did."

This couldn't happen. I had enough sense to realize that kissing Jareth was the first step toward becoming irrevocably attached to him in a way that would destroy me once he eventually left. That didn't mean I had the will power or even the strength to pull away from him. His lips hovered over mine and his light blue eyes took on that otherworldly glow again. Just as I was about to succumb to the inevitability of our lips melding into the kind of kiss that curls your toes and leaves you breathless, a loud knocking rapped against the door.

I jumped out of his arms as if he'd scalded me with his powers. The impassioned look he gave me certainly made me think he intended to. Feeling grateful for the reprieve, I hurried to the door and opened it.

"Hi there, Crysta, do you think I could trouble you for some cat food?" Mrs. Armijo asked.

I smiled at my neighbor from across the hall, a tiny woman who owned more cats than was legal.

"Sure. I actually bought an extra bag for you."

Her watery blue eyes twinkled merrily. The skin around them wrinkled like thin tissue paper as she gave me a grateful smile.

"You know me so well. I always run out of cat food

about this time of the month, don't I?"

I nodded and invited her in. The moment she caught a glimpse of Jareth, her eyes narrowed. That old lady drank him in from head to toe.

"I didn't know you had a boyfriend, Crysta."

"Well, I don't have…"

"Does he always dress like that?" she said in a loud whisper.

I awkwardly cleared my throat and walked into the kitchen. Within seconds I had the bag of cat food in hand. I almost didn't want to return to the living room. Once my neighbor left, I was afraid Jareth would want to pick up right where we left off. Facing the inevitable, I walked back in, gave her the bag, and ushered her to the door, but she wasn't quite ready to take her leave. Just as she reached the threshold she turned around and gave him a serious look.

"Crysta, is a darling little creature. I assume you plan on taking care of her?"

"It was really nice to see you again," I told her as I tried to push her out the door. She outmaneuvered me and soon I was the one standing on the threshold.

Jareth's amusement was palpable as he took in Mrs. Armijo

"I do intend to provide for her every want and need," he assured her.

She nodded her approval then turned to me and said, "I'd marry that hunka hunka burnin' love immediately if I were you. You can always buy him a pair of jeans later." She gave me a sweet smile as she walked out the door. "See you next week."

I closed the door behind her and cursed my flushed cheeks.

"You were going to tell her I wasn't your boyfriend?" he

said. It almost sounded like an accusation.

My eyes flew to him in confusion.

"That's right."

"Why?"

"Because it's the truth."

"Is it?"

His eyes held mine for a few intense moments. It was far longer and more emotionally charged than I was comfortable with. I lowered my gaze and skirted around him, hoping to make it past the kitchen entrance before he tried to inflict any more consequences upon my person.

"Where are you going?" he asked. "We still have plenty of practicing to do...among other things." The sultry tone of his voice hinted at all of those other things he wanted to practice. I needed a cold shower and possibly a bottle of sleeping pills.

"I'm going to the bathroom. I require a brief lady's moment."

"What's a lady's moment?"

"I gotta pee."

His bark of laughter followed me down the hallway.

"A female faerie would never announce her intent to relieve herself," he shouted.

My shoulders relaxed a little as the tension between us dispersed.

"I guess it's a good thing I'm not a faerie then, isn't it?"

He didn't answer, but I got the feeling my response had displeased him in some way. It was obvious he cared for me, at least enough to stick around and make sure I wasn't wrongfully assassinated. How thoughtful, really, but no amount of caring was going to change the fact that I was human, a member of a species for which he held little regard.

I was human, and he was a faerie. Kissing him was a

very stupid thing to do.

Yep. Absolutely crazy.

After using the restroom and seeing my reflection in the mirror, I was even more determined to get to the store and grab that hair-dye. I stuck my head out of the bathroom and yelled down the hall.

"Hey, Jareth, where did my purse end up? And please don't tell me it got left behind in Santo...wherever we traveled to."

"Your hand bag with its various compartments is safe and sound on your coffee table," he said. "A curious thing to be carrying around. You know you could simply store your monetary devices in a different dimension and call upon them when needed, don't you?"

"Seriously? Why would I know something like that?" I said as I began to walk down the hall. "And furthermore," I muttered to myself, "how in the world would I accomplish something like that?"

A soft padded sound alerted my sensitive ears to the possibility of someone standing behind me. Did Jareth transport himself down the hall?

I swiftly turned around, ready to smack him for sneaking up on me again.

"Jareth, you really need to stop—"

A sharp jab to my stomach knocked the wind out of me and sent me flying against the wall. I glanced up in shock only to discover a man who looked a lot like Jareth grab a knife from his belt and take a step forward.

I wanted to scream for help, but I was still fighting for some air. I sank to the floor as oxygen finally flooded my lungs.

"For Jareth," he stated in a soft whisper, raising the dagger high.

I dug deep within my frozen core, lifted my hand, and

shot a frosty blast of air at the intruder's face, hoping to disorient him for a moment. Just as I called the frozen shards forward and threw them from my hand, a blast of air shot the man back down the hallway.

"Nuallan," Jareth yelled. "Stand down." He stood over me with his hands clenched at his sides, anger burning his features. Bending low, he grabbed me by the arm and gently lifted me to my feet. He pressed me behind him in a protective gesture, but I peeked my head around his broad frame anyway and stared at the man who was now getting to his feet, an expression of shock enshrouding his features.

"Jareth." He went to one knee and lowered his head in a gesture of submission or possibly respect.

I seriously had no idea what to think at this point.

"Why have you come here, Nuallan, and why did you take it upon yourself to fulfill my assignment?"

"Assignment?" I said in outrage. "Are you referring to the assignment you were given to kill me? Just how many people is your chancellor planning on sending to my apartment?"

"Crysta. Please. Allow me to handle this."

"You are protecting the mark?" Nuallan asked. His incredulity was nearly comical. "Jareth, when you failed to return and report your findings we all feared the worst. We thought for certain the target you were sent to assassinate had managed to kill you instead."

"Do you truly believe me to be so weak?" Jareth bellowed in outrage.

"Hey," I shouted. "This is the second time in two days I've had an assassin show up uninvited in my apartment and try to kill me."

"I merely threatened to kill you," Jareth corrected.

"Semantics," I muttered as I came around him and

planted myself in front of Jareth. He let out a dissatisfied grunt. I pointed a finger at his colleague. "I happen to be a very nice person who tends to avoid random acts of murder and mayhem. You have two seconds to apologize for punching me in the stomach with intent to stab me to death."

"You punched her in the stomach?" Jareth yelled.

"I thought she killed you. I was merely avenging your death and fulfilling your assignment."

"Oh for heaven's sake, both of you just shut up." Their surprised faces took me in. "Are you hungry?" I asked pointing to Nuallan.

He looked more than a little discombobulated with the question. "Well...I..."

"Fabulous. I'm starving to death, and I need to go grab some more hair-dye at the store. How about we all walk to the local Wal-Mart and get some lunch?"

I turned without waiting for a response, headed for the living room, and picked up my purse from the coffee table. I turned around once I reached the door only to discover that they were still standing in the hallway.

"Are you two faeries coming or not? Because I plan on leaving with or without you."

Jareth finally cracked a smile and turned to his Fae friend. "Come, Nuallan. I promise you, the young lady will make good on her threat."

"I'll come, but I am most confused at this turn of events, Your Majesty."

"Your Majesty? Geez. You weren't kidding when you asked me to use that title," I said.

"A simple human would be so favored as to be given the honor of addressing our prince as Your Majesty," Nuallan said in a hostile tone.

I quirked an eyebrow at Jareth. "First you're an

assassin, then you're a member of the Fae, and now you're royalty. Curiouser and curiouser," I said.

And with that I opened the door and walked through it, positive that my two Fae companions would be quick to follow.

Chapter Six

Our dining area resembled that of a McDonald's restaurant. Okay, so it basically *was* a McDonald's restaurant tightly ensconced within a Super Wal-Mart.

Super glamorous.

I'd gone straight for the fruit bowl and a container of nuts in the produce section, while my two companions did the same. Nuallan had refused to say anything to me during our four block sojourn to the store. Instead, he'd repeatedly said things *about* me as if I wasn't walking a few feet ahead of them. After he'd accused me of being a witch and the worst kind of threat to their harmonious empire, Jareth threatened to cut his tongue out if he didn't shut up.

A little harsh in my opinion, but the silence was most welcome.

Now that we were sitting at a tiny table in McDonald's, stuffing our faces with fruits, nuts and tofu—the direct antithesis of all that McDonald's stood for—Jareth seemed ready to discuss the elephant in the room.

"You were sent to kill Crysta even though I had not reported on my progress," he said.

Nuallan chewed his food for a moment and then

69

swallowed. I studied the tense lines around his mouth and jaw. He was just as well-muscled and intimidating as Jareth. His long, white hair and strange green tunic looked completely foreign in my world.

They both did.

"With all due respect, Your Majesty, you failed to report your progress in the time allotted, and the chancellor feared the worst."

Jareth barked a scoffing laugh. "You all surmised that a simple human had the power to overcome me? Kill me?"

"Hey, this simple human knows some sweet karate moves from several months of self-defense classes," I said. "I'm like a ninja when I want to be."

Jareth turned to me and laid a warm hand over mine. "Yes, you're quite intimidating, Crysta. The most challenging assignment I've ever been given." He winked at me and I shook my head, fighting the smile that teased the corners of my mouth.

"You've been a real pain in the arse ever since you showed up in my apartment yesterday. You know that?"

He laughed. "I'm assuming that's another of your lovely human expressions?"

"I can think of an even lovelier one if you'd like to hear it."

Nuallan dropped his food and stared at us in amazement. "You've befriended the mark. You...you actually like her. The threat to our monarchy...to the king himself, is seated before us and you have become besotted with her rather than do your duty and protect your king. My Lord, I fail to understand the reasoning behind this."

Jareth cast an annoyed glance at his assassin friend. "She may be a threat to the monarchy, but not in the way you might think."

I had no idea what he was talking about, but since we

were all crazy freaks in our own unique way, I waited to see what his explanation might be. I also took careful note of the fact that he hadn't bothered to deny that he was besotted with me. I couldn't help but hope that might be the case.

"Pay attention to what happens when I take down her glamour," Jareth said.

"Glamour? You've been masking my presence?"

"Just toning it down a bit. There haven't been any men following you around over the last hour or so, right?"

"Well, I haven't made eye-contact with any of them."

"Do so with the young man at the register." He pointed to a red-headed kid about my age, scrubbing down the counter before him.

I narrowed my brows, my mouth drawing into a thin line. "I don't need another stalker, Jareth. You and this idiot you have here is all I can handle at the moment."

Nuallan stiffened his posture, but Jareth laid a hand on his shoulder, barely stifling the laughter at my comment.

"Just make eye-contact with him, Crysta."

I shook my head, knowing this was a bad idea, but did what he asked anyway. I stood up and walked over to the register, flashing what I hoped was a killer smile, something that felt completely foreign to me considering the situation.

"Hey, there. Do you think I could get some ketchup packets, please?" The young man looked up and immediately froze. The moment his eyes met mine, his pupils dilated and the color in his face heightened.

*Here we go.*

"Oh...y-y-yes. Of course you can." He rushed to the side and ducked under, grabbing several ketchup packets and reaching across the counter to hand them to me. I allowed his fingertips to gently make contact with my

71

hand, and his color heightened even further.

Thanking him, I accepted the packets and turned around, taking note of Nuallan's amazed expression and Jareth's self-satisfied grin. They didn't understand what I'd just done. What events I had just put in motion. It wouldn't be long before the young man did something absolutely...

A soft tug on my arm alerted me to the worker's presence. I turned to face him, recognizing the strange, obsessive glint in his eye.

"If you're not doing anything after I get off work, I'd like to take you out to dinner."

I swallowed hard, feeling sick to my stomach. "I'm sorry, but I have other plans for the evening. Thank you anyway."

My attempt to move around him was thwarted. He blocked my way, placing a possessive hand at my waist. "I'll take you out to eat now, then. I can leave whenever I want."

Just as I was about to use those mad ninja skills I'd only recently bragged about, Jareth stepped forward and gently pulled me out of the guy's arms.

"She's taken, friend." He then said a few words that sounded more like gibberish, and the most amazing thing happened. The young man's fevered look became normal again and he took a step back. He looked a little confused for a moment, but then shook his head and walked back to his station behind the counter.

I looked at Jareth in stunned surprise.

"How in the world did you do that?"

"I put your glamour back on."

"What exactly does this glamour do, and why would I need it?"

"By King Moridan's golden crown, she's Fae," Nuallan

whispered.

My eyes widened in shock, but I immediately disregarded that ridiculous notion.

"Nope. I'm definitely not Fae. I was born human to two very human parents who died in a very stupid car crash, and then I spent the next fifteen years in and out of very human foster homes. So, nope. Not Fae," I said.

"Of course you are!" Nuallan stated, still sounding shocked at what I considered to be a flawed assumption. "Only our female faeries have that kind of effect on human men."

"Not Fae," I repeated stubbornly. There were about a half dozen explanations as to why I had the effect I did on the human male species—like pheromones, or a very unfortunate case of bad luck—but being a faerie wasn't a possibility I was willing to entertain. Totally ludicrous.

I walked over to our table, sat down, and threw some nuts into my mouth.

"And her name is Crysta," Jareth continued, seating himself again. He and Nuallan shared an annoyingly significant look. I didn't like it one bit.

"That's very interesting," Nuallan said.

I slapped my hand on the table. "I keep hearing that. Why is everything about me so interesting?"

"Crysta, don't you see the similarities between us?"

I gave him a blank look. I didn't want to accept what he and his friend were getting at. I didn't want to believe that my parents weren't really my parents or that I was quite possibly more of a freak than I'd ever before considered.

"If your suspicions are correct, Jareth, then there are dark forces at work among the ruling classes, and Crysta won't be safe until we discover who ordered her death both now and seventeen years ago."

"You guys put a hit out on me when I was a baby?" I

looked at them both in disgust. "You people are sick."

"No, Crysta. This is more complicated than you can imagine. This is a mystery that has plagued the Fae realm for many years," Nuallan explained.

"What mystery?"

Jareth placed a calming hand on mine, but kept his focus on Nuallan.

"I need you to return and report that you accomplished your mission and murdered the mark. You mustn't tell anyone, not even my father, what is truly going on. I'm not sure how far this treachery reaches, but I don't want my father's life endangered by revealing to him what could be explosive information."

"Explosive indeed," Nuallan said, staring at the hand Jareth left resting upon mine. I looked down and noticed the effervescent light created with our skin-to-skin contact.

"Do you have any idea what that light means?" Nuallan asked.

"It's a curiosity I've started looking into."

"Allow me to save you the trouble. I have two words for you. Fated mates. And a possible winter faerie if our suspicions are correct. Has it occurred to you that this may be why the family was murdered?"

Jareth's jaw clenched in anger while I sat there like an ignoramus waiting for someone to shed some light on whatever the hell it was they were getting at.

"If it is, there will be serious repercussions for those who were and apparently still are involved," Jareth said. The steely flint of his voice gave me the shivers. It was one of the few times I saw the cold, calculating warrior lurking beneath.

"Okay, since neither one of you intends to fill me in on what's happening, I'm going to go grab some hair-dye and then we can get going."

74

"Hair-dye? Is that what you've been using to cover your hair?" Jareth asked, refusing to release my hand. He had a bad habit of doing that.

"Oh, you noticed my roots, huh?" I hated how self-conscious I sounded.

"Of course, I did. They're white, like mine. Why have you been covering your hair up with this strange honey color?" Surprisingly, he released my hand and reached toward the back of my head, pulling out the scrunchie binding my hair.

"Hey. Could you please get on board with the concept of personal space?"

"She may be Fae, but she talks in riddles," Nuallan muttered, eying my hair as Jareth ran his soft fingers through it.

"Once again, I am not Fae. I'm human. And the color of my hair is a freaky birth defect I have gone to great lengths to cover up."

"It's definitely something you were born with, but I'd hardly call it a defect. It's exactly the same color as mine and Nuallan's."

I don't know why his statement was such a shocking revelation. I had already taken note of their unnatural hair color, but I hadn't considered our hair being alike for several reasons.

One, it had been some time since I'd actually taken a look at my real hair color. The minute the dye washed out, I hurried to apply more color.

Two, no one on this planet looked like me, and believe me, I'd searched for distinctive features and similarities— anything that might explain my own origins and strange birth defects, i.e., albino skin, overly large, slanted blue eyes, ears that came to a soft point. I felt ugly, to say the least.

Three, no matter how delusional Jareth was, he was also beautifully built. Every line and angle of his face, all the curves and edges of his body must have been constructed for the pure enjoyment of the female species. I would never have considered any feature of mine to be comparable to his.

"It's not the same," I said, swallowing hard and folding my arms against my chest.

"It is." He placed his hands upon mine again. My eyes locked with his, but in my peripheral vision, I could see white light rising just beneath the contact of our skin.

"Your hair is like mine, your eyes are like mine, you smell of pine and wintergreen."

I shook my head in stubborn denial, angry to have him point out all the reasons I'd been a less-than-desirable addition to any and all families everywhere.

"Fascinating, Jareth." I gave those two words as much sarcasm as I could muster. "Now if you two will excuse me, I've got a date with a bottle of dye."

For once, Jareth released me. No doubt the panicked look on my face led him to realize that I was starting to lose it.

"How do you understand the creature?" Nuallan asked as I turned to leave.

I quickly put distance between us and hurried toward the cosmetics area of the store, finding the right box in a matter of seconds—I'd been at it for several years now—and paying for it as quickly as possible. I didn't want to return to Jareth and his opinionated comrade. I didn't want to analyze what all of these experiments and revelations might mean for my own future or my own identity.

I was human. I was just like everyone else. I belonged here and I'd fought hard to carve out a place in this world for myself. No freaky hallucination or opinionated, self-important faerie prince was going to ruin my peace of mind. Not if I had anything to say about it.

After hovering near the checkout line, I decided I was going to assert my independence right then and there. I wasn't Jareth's lackey, servant, or subject, and I certainly wasn't his prisoner. I was an independent woman who had the right to return home on her own if she wanted to. And that is exactly what I determined to do. I turned toward the opposite exit, walked through the doors, and headed out into the light afternoon sunshine, grateful for the charm Jareth had placed upon me since I hadn't had the chance to put sunscreen on before we left.

I then made the short trek home, completely unconcerned with what Jareth might think once I failed to return.

Chapter Seven

I'd barely walked through the door before an infuriated Jareth materialized right inside my living room.

"Seriously? I totally forgot you could do that. I thought I'd have at least a few minutes of peace before you came to find me."

Jareth strode across the room and grabbed my shoulders. I nearly dropped my bag of precious hair-dye.

"Do you have any idea how dangerous and reckless it was for you to wander off like that?"

My mouth dropped open in surprise.

"Wander off? Are you really going to stand there and talk to me like I'm three years old? According to the state of California, I'm considered an adult, and I've been coming and going without having to report to anyone for a really long time now."

He bit the bottom of his lip, quite possibly to stave off some angry words, but it was super distracting.

"It's dangerous for you to be alone right now."

"I don't see why. You put a glamour on me. I haven't picked up any new stalker friends, and Nuallan is off to report my death to your Fae monarch, whom I'm assuming is your father. How about that family dynamic?

78

Right?"

Jareth wasn't even remotely amused.

"There's a contract out on your life. We can't know for certain how long Nuallan's story will hold up. We also have no idea if Nuallan was the only assassin the monarchy sent. You could have been killed walking home on your own."

"Once again you doubt my mad ninja skills and it's really starting to hurt my feelings."

"Crysta," Jareth warned.

I pushed away from him. I needed space and clarity and less disapproval from a guy who I no longer believed to be a hallucination. Which meant all of this was real. I didn't feel equipped to embrace this new reality.

"Anything could happen to me any day of the week, Jareth. My life hasn't exactly been all honey and roses. I understand danger, and I'm fairly good at avoiding it."

"But you weren't prepared for me or Nuallan, and you won't be prepared for the next assassin they send." He came up behind me and placed his hands upon my shoulders with a little more gentleness this time. He eased me back to lean against his chest where I easily succumbed to the security his embrace offered me.

Dang it.

"Please, Crysta, I don't mean to treat you as if you are incompetent, but when you didn't return it frightened me. An awful foreboding took root deep within me. I don't normally fear anything, but I'm terrified of losing you."

My breath hitched in my throat. I had *not* expected that kind of admission from the prince of the Fae. Granted, I'd never seen him in his element, but I could only imagine how many faerie women were vying for his attentions. The thought quite literally sickened me.

That was a bad sign.

79

Then I considered how ludicrous it was to take his meaning as anything other than concern for a friend and someone he had sworn to protect. I'd never been anything special to anyone, and there was no need to assume that my status would change anytime soon. Especially with a prince.

Geez, he really was a prince. No wonder the dude was so bossy.

"It's fine." I took in a deep breath and forced myself to step out of his embrace. No sense in getting used to something that couldn't last for long. As soon as Jareth believed the threat to my safety had been dealt with, he'd probably take off to destinations foreign and unimaginable. A world I'd only ever heard of in fairy tales.

*He* was a fairy tale, and I needed someone in my life who didn't have the power to disapparate whenever he felt like it.

"Look, I really need to go cover up my hair and start filling out more job applications."

"No."

I turned around to face him, wondering which part of that sentence he had just vetoed. He had his arms folded across his chest and his lips had thinned into a displeased grimace.

"What's the problem now?"

"You can't color your hair. It isn't right. Changing the natural color of your hair is like dismissing who you are and where you come from."

I was too emotionally drained to have this conversation.

"I know who I am. My name is Crysta Jensen. I was born June 7, 1999 to Leslie and Carter Jensen. When I was six months old they died in a car accident and thus began my illustrious career in foster care. Several months ago, by some crazy miracle, I became emancipated and moved into a shelter until I found a roommate—"

"You moved into a shelter?" His eyebrows drew together in puzzlement.

"Yeees. Is that a problem for you? You were expecting me to have gone straight to a palace as majestic and lovely as yours most likely is?"

"I've studied your court system extensively over the years, and there is absolutely no way a judge would have ruled emancipation in your favor unless you had an actual home and some proof of income that demonstrated your ability to provide for yourself. From what I've seen over the last two days, you are woefully incapable of even paying for your rent, let alone your food. And a shelter? That's the only home you had to offer the court as proof of your stability?"

"I'm getting super tired of being treated like an incapable ignoramus—"

"Crysta, you're missing my point. A normal judge who intended to abide by these strict laws would never have allowed you to take care of yourself."

"Why not?" I cried out. "I've been taking care of myself all these years anyway. My foster families didn't love me, they didn't provide for me, and in some situations they didn't even provide a room or a bed for me. Sleeping in the cellar was a real treat, Jareth."

He held up his hands in a placating gesture as I took in deep breaths to try and calm the angry storm that threatened to erupt from within me.

"What I am trying to impress upon you is this, the judge who ruled in your favor did so to make you more vulnerable. It's much easier to assassinate your mark when they are on their own rather than surrounded by family. Who would take notice if a recently emancipated orphan suddenly disappeared?"

My eyes widened at the implications of this revelation.

"You've been marked for death for quite some time, Crysta. It makes me wonder how long these people have been planning this."

"Well, according to you and Nuallan, seventeen years."

"Yes, but seventeen years ago someone actually succeeded in killing you."

"That makes absolutely no sense."

He ran a frustrated hand through his long, white hair.

"They killed someone they thought was you. All this time you've been alive and somehow they recently discovered their mistake and wished to correct it. And the disturbing part of this entire debacle is that it came from the highest levels of our kingdom."

"Why am I such a threat, Jareth? Why? I am nobody. I'm nothing special."

Jareth's eyes zeroed in on me and then softened as he took in my anguished expression. He reached forward and brushed some hair away from my face.

"If only you realized just how special you are. Even if you were only human you would be extraordinary, but being what you are—and who I suspect you really are—makes you that much more unique and precious, especially to me."

"So we're back to who I am, huh?" My half-hearted attempt at easing the seriousness of the moment failed miserably. He didn't even crack a smile. He just inched his way closer and took my free hand in his.

His dark blue eyes drew me in and promised me all sorts of things I'd always desired and knew could never be mine. A girl could easily lose herself in promises like that, but my experiences had proved to me that promises were easily made and even more easily broken. I stepped away and took in a deep breath. A clear head was the only thing preventing me from begging Jareth to care for me as more than just his self-appointed charge.

"There's a few DVDs and basic cable you can watch while I'm in the bathroom."

"While you're in the bathroom covering your hair?"

I swallowed hard. Why did this bother him so badly? Why did I actually care whether he disapproved or not?

For heaven's sake, it was my hair, my life, and my choice. I wanted to fit in, not stand out. I wanted to blend into the crowd and just be normal. I jutted out my chin and squared my shoulders.

"Yes."

He gave me a resigned smile and nodded. Then he stepped forward and bent low to give me a gentle kiss on my forehead.

"Either way, you'll still look beautiful," he whispered. His warm breath and calming scent nearly wrecked my resolve.

Then he turned around and walked over to the coffee table. I watched in wonder as the faerie prince sat himself down on my grungy sofa and picked up the remote control.

He studied it for a few moments and pushed the red button at the top. The TV came on and his eyes widened in surprise as a football game unfolded on the screen.

"Humans may be primitive barbarians, but I do enjoy many of their technological discoveries. I read about this sport during my studies. What is this violent activity called again?"

"Football."

"Why? They rarely touch the ball with their feet. The more appropriate term would be handball."

"You, Europe, and South America share that same

grievance."

I let out a chuckle as I headed down the hallway. I tried not to think about the sad look in Jareth's eyes as I entered the bathroom.

Chapter Eight

Once my hair had been dyed and dried to perfection, I walked back into the living room and stood in shock at the sight of Jareth sitting on the floor in front of the TV watching the New York ballet's production of *Swan Lake* on PBS.

"You like ballet too?"

Jareth jumped at the sound of my voice and swiveled around. He took in my newly dyed roots for a moment, but refrained from saying anything for which I was grateful.

Instead he said, "I have found many human forms of dance truly magnificent, but your ballets remind me very much of the way our Fae women dance in our realm. Our people have even gone so far as to incorporate ballet choreography in our dance festivals."

I sat down next to him and we watched the graceful leaps and lifts of the corps de ballet. A flood of recognition hit me when the principal dancer came leaping onto the stage with her partner.

"Oh, look. It's Monique," I squealed.

Jareth turned to me in surprise.

"You know this particular dancer?"

85

I nodded, never taking my eyes off her perfect lines and flawless technique.

"Well, we're more acquaintances than anything else. I met her at a dance festival here in San Diego. All of the ballet companies in the USA came together and took turns performing. I've been taking ballet for years and know about all of the different principal dancers in many different companies. Monique has been my favorite for a while."

"I didn't know you danced," Jareth said with interest. "How appropriate that you chose ballet when you could have chosen any other form of dance, wouldn't you say?"

His not so subtle hint irritated me.

"So when I heard about the festival," I continued, "I saved my money for tickets and went to every show I could."

"And that's how you met this Monique?"

I finally peeled my eyes from the TV and looked at his amused expression.

"What?"

"Nothing. It's just that this person has brought more color and excitement to your face than I've seen since my arrival."

"When you broke in, you mean?"

"Technically, I apparated."

"Without permission, but since you've saved my life twice now, I'm going to let it slide."

"Let what slide? In which direction?"

"It's slang, Jareth." I rolled my eyes heavenward. "I really need you to assimilate here. Anyway, I sneaked backstage after the last performance. I wanted to meet Monique so badly, but I guess she never went out after the performances to sign autographs or mingle with the guests. Not a fan of the crowds, maybe." I could so relate.

I studied her movements as her partner lifted her into a graceful leap. "I found her dressing room and totally barged in. I think my youth and star-struck expression got me out of trouble because she laughed at the intrusion and gave me a big hug. I remember it so well because her embrace felt like coming home. It wasn't a feeling I was used to."

"That's interesting. So out of all the humans you've ever come in contact with, this particular human made you feel as if you belonged?"

I startled at how perfectly Jareth had nailed it.

"Yep. She felt like home. She felt like you."

I clenched my jaw, furious with myself for having let that little admission slip.

He was gracious enough to not comment on it.

"You had that one meeting with her, and that was the end of your time together?"

"No. She invited me to go eat lunch with her the following day before her company left for New York. I couldn't believe it. We had fruit salads and talked for hours about her career as a dancer and the amazing places she'd traveled to. I was sorry to see her go."

"Do you keep in touch?"

"We email each other sometimes, but she's pretty busy, and I'm always working."

Jareth stared at the screen, but his look was more analytical than anything else.

"What?" I asked.

"The more I watch her dance, the more otherworldly she seems to me. Don't you think it's possible that she isn't human?"

"I know you hate humans, but you need to quit turning humans into faeries, Jareth. She's perfectly normal."

"And yet she dances like she's Fae."

"I don't even know what that means."

"You said she felt like home. Like me. There's a reason for that. You feel a sense of kinship with your own people."

"Nuallan didn't make me feel that way."

Jareth laughed hard at that.

"No. I suppose the threat of your death prevented you from relaxing in his presence."

I quirked a smile and continued to watch Monique as she glided and leaped across the floor, twirling in her partner's arms one minute and then lightly dancing upon her toes the next. All that movement appeared so easy for her, but I understood the dedication and hard work it took to achieve something that looked so effortless. My insides ached for Monday to arrive and my ballet class to begin. I seriously hated the weekends. I took my regular ballet classes on Mondays and Wednesdays, and company classes were Tuesdays and Thursdays. Thoughts of my auditions coming up made my insides quake with anticipation. Thoughts of how I was going to pay for everything if I actually succeeded in joining the San Diego Ballet brought me back to reality.

I sighed and stood, heading for my room to fill out more job applications.

"You don't have to work, you know."

Geez. It was like he could read my mind.

I turned to him as he lifted himself from the floor and walked toward me.

"Of course I do. How am I going to pay the rent?"

"I'm paying for it. Remember? I'm your new co-habitor now."

"Co-habitor?" I smiled. "Yeah. We'll see what Jami has to say about it."

"Jamie has already been taken care of."

He must have noticed my alarmed expression because he was quick to reassure me that he hadn't killed her—just spelled her to move back in with her mother.

"Haven't you noticed all her things are gone?"

"First of all, I haven't even been in her room. So no. I didn't notice. Plus, this TV and coffee table are hers. You weren't planning on returning them?"

"How was I supposed to know they were hers?" he shrugged.

"When did you have time to spell my roommate and move her out?"

"Last night. I left some protective wards around you and took care of business. Now we have the apartment all to ourselves. Just the two of us." He took a step closer and gave me a wide grin. Heaven help me, but it was the sexiest grin a Fae assassin had ever given.

Pretty sure, anyway.

I swallowed hard. "Cozy."

He closed the distance between us but didn't immediately reach for my hair like he usually did.

"Very," he whispered.

Dang it. Did this stupid faerie have to reduce me to an inarticulate puddle of goo with his sophisticated charm and yummy masculinity?

Annoying.

"I need you to put your own glamour back on," I said in a tight voice.

"Faeries don't need glamours when they are in each other's presence. We only have that overpowering effect on humans."

"I'm human."

"We won't argue that point again, but maybe you should begin to entertain the idea that the pull you feel toward me is completely organic rather than some unnatural compulsion."

"Why would I want to admit something like that?"

"Because then I would know I'm not the only one feeling like this."

"Like what?"

"Like holding you in my arms and kissing you is the only thing that makes sense right now."

I swear my heart was beating right out of my chest at that moment, but any romantic inclinations his words produced were easily squelched when I considered how awful it was going to be to say good-bye to him. Any physical bond we created would only make our good-byes a million times worse.

"I think that's a very bad idea."

"Why?"

"Because I'm not really someone you can have a relationship with. You can't exactly bring me home to dear old dad, especially with this threat hanging over my head. Plus, you're a prince. Isn't there some type of dating protocol you have to follow or an arranged marriage you're supposed to willingly jump into?"

He shook his head and folded his arms across his chest in disapproval.

"You are the only person I can have a relationship with. Don't you see it, Crysta? Every particle of my being recognizes yours."

I panicked at the hope his words produced. I did not need this eventual devastating level of disappointment.

"That's some line, Jareth. What else did you watch while I was dyeing my hair?"

He grunted and stepped forward, enfolding my hands in his.

"Once again, I have no idea what you're talking about, but from your tone of voice it would seem you don't believe me, or at the very least you completely mistake my meaning." He held our connected hands up, allowing the glow from our contact to brighten the space between us.

"When we touch, our essence heats and connects, fracturing light from our cells and distributing it on the surface, creating an otherworldly glow."

"Okay, thanks for that entirely unromantic scientific explanation."

"Yes, I must admit that at first this particular phenomenon completely puzzled me."

"Just this one, huh? I've been beyond puzzled for like, two days now. Why has this issue caught your attention?"

He slid his hands down the length of my arms, trailing hot, white light as he went. Then he placed them both at the small of my back, drawing me closer and forcing me to position my hands against his sturdy chest. So far, denial had been a fairly effective emotional move, but all of this supernatural, otherworldly stuff had worn me down.

"It caught my attention due to its significance. It's the reason I changed my mind about killing you."

"For which I'm eternally grateful."

His yummy lips lifted into an adorable smile.

"I'm not doing this right. I treated you like the enemy, threatened to kill you, and then moved in uninvited. I'm not exactly wooing you successfully, am I?"

"I didn't know you were trying."

He chuckled. "Then you've confirmed my worst fears. The females in my previous relationships weren't nearly as feisty, outspoken, or as unimpressed with me as you seem to be."

"Please refrain from talking about other relationships in my presence. It's nauseating."

"I'm very glad to hear that."

I glared at him and the self-satisfied smirk that spread

across his face.

"How about you explain to me what this," I grabbed his hands from my waist and lifted them in front of his face where the glow illuminated his perfect features, "means for you and me."

He nodded, focusing again on our previous conversation.

"Members of the Seely Court, more specifically, royalty, will have this kind of physical reaction to their fated mate until the time they are united through an important ceremony, though this doesn't happen very often. A prince of the Seely Court hasn't found a fated mate in close to a thousand years, and yet, here I am, having this reaction with you."

"Prince of the Seely Court, eh? Why are you an assassin if you're supposed to rule the Fae realm someday?"

"It's part of my training. I won't be ready to lead my people for another five hundred years. The current king, my father, still has much to teach me." He shook his head, "My being a prince isn't really the issue at the moment. The fact of the matter is this: from the first moment we touched and produced this physical and chemical reaction with one another, I knew you couldn't be human, but I didn't know for certain what you were or how we could be reacting to one another in such a magnificent way. It simply isn't possible since there are no available females within the Seely Court who also bear the mark of royalty."

"So what race did you believe me to be?"

"A witch, perhaps, but based on all of my other observations and experiments, it's clear to me that you have to be a member of the Fae."

"Oh, yes. Crystal clear." There was nothing clear about it. All my life, I'd never fit in with my fellow man, but I'd always assumed I was one of them. I felt an identity crisis of epic proportions coming on.

"But on that score, there are a few more things that are troubling me. A few more details that don't add up."

"I'm all ears."

He smiled. "That's it exactly. I'm almost positive you're Fae, but your ears are blunted and round, not pointed like mine. You see?" He used one hand to pull his hair back. I nearly did a double take when I saw his beautifully pointed ears.

"Mine used to be pointed like that, but I had them filed down," I stated.

Jareth looked at me in horror. "Filed down? You mean, you had someone surgically round your ears on purpose? By the gods, why would you do something so degrading to yourself?"

I pulled my hand out of his and moved past him toward the center of the room. His disapproval was hard to handle head on.

"Not that it's any of your business, but it was another birth defect preventing me from being adopted by warm, fuzzy families willing to love their children unconditionally...so long as their ears looked normal."

I'd wanted plastic surgery for most of my life and had spent years saving up enough money to get rid of the pointed tips. I thought that by changing my appearance, I would change the way prospective parents viewed me. I thought it might make them love me. It had been two years since I'd had the surgery, and nothing had changed, not even my poor self-esteem.

"You removed your most beautiful, defining features so humans would love you?"

The thunderous look in Jareth's eyes made me wonder why I'd bothered to explain myself. I doubted he'd ever been hard-pressed to find love and acceptance.

"No one wanted me. Don't you get that? I needed to be just like everyone else."

He walked over and reached for the tip of my right ear, running his finger along the curved portion of it. It sent a delicious chill down my spine.

"And conforming to other people's definitions of what normal is…of what beauty is—essentially deforming yourself—was the only solution you could come up with?"

I sighed and steered the discussion in a different direction.

"You said there were several things puzzling you."

It took a moment for Jareth to respond. He was still rubbing the tip of my ear with his thumb and forefinger, no doubt trying to get the point to grow back.

It was nice.

Nice and crazy!

"This entire situation is one large puzzle due to the type of faerie you actually are," he said, finally aborting his attempts to fix my ear. "You're not a member of the Seely Court. You're a winter faerie."

I let out a tired moan. My head was spinning with every new delusional revelation.

"You know, I really should be in my room filling out job applications, but I'll stay here and humor you a little while longer. If I'm a winter faerie, what are you exactly?"

"I'm Jareth, prince of the Seely Court and ruler of the summer faeries. Take away the titles and accolades, and I'm merely a summer faerie. That's why this whole situation is so perplexing. Finding one's mate is rare enough, but a mating between a summer and a winter faerie—and both of them royalty at that—is unprecedented. I've never read nor heard any instance of this in the centuries I've studied our history."

"That's because all of this is absolutely crazy, Jareth! I can barely wrap my head around the fact that you're a faerie prince, and now you're telling me I'm faerie royalty as well? I'm not a faerie. I'm not a member of the Fae. We're not fated to be together. In fact, I'd much rather believe that you're just a crazy person who managed to find his way into my apartment, sucking me into one insane delusion after another." I took in a deep breath and let it out slowly when Jareth gave me an exasperated look.

"Then how do you explain the light we create and the pull we feel toward one another?"

"What pull? I don't feel a pull!" The lie felt ugly and wrong the minute it left my lips.

Jareth gave me a small smirk. "You're just as taken with me as I am with you."

"That's really why you decided to spare me, isn't it? You think I'm hot!"

His look was quizzical. "Hot? Of course not. You're a winter faerie. You're cold-blooded by nature."

I wearily rested my head against his chest and felt heat blossom within me from the contact. "There has to be a slang dictionary somewhere on Amazon. Just so you know, I plan on using *your* money to purchase it for you." He placed a hand against the back of my neck and began to massage the millions of stress-induced knots. Neck massages from a gorgeous faerie prince assassin.

Yeah. Just par for the course at this point.

"What makes you think I'm a winter faerie?" I asked in a strained voice.

"Crysta, you blasted me with ice and froze my arms the first night I was here. It is a common defensive move that most winter faeries learn in their infancy. Then there's your skin. It's pure white and it burns and blisters within a few minutes of exposure to intense sunlight. It's the kind of reaction a faerie with strong ties to the seasonal elements of winter produces. And only royals are so strongly tied to the elements."

I lifted my head quickly and stepped back a little, though the movement did nothing to loosen his hold on me. "Yes, but I can handle the sun in less intense climates."

"Most winter faeries can as well. Your body temperature is ice cold. I'm guessing you rarely feel the cold in winter."

"I usually try not to feel anything, Jareth." He was dead right, though, and it made me super nervous.

"Your emotions are directly tied to your powers. Whenever you feel threatened, you are capable of freezing your attacker's heart momentarily, giving you enough time to flee."

I swallowed hard at this. I'd never really understood what it was I did when protecting myself from some of my slime ball foster fathers. I'd merely push them away and they would freeze up while grasping their chests. I think I'd spent most of my life blaming their reactions on high cholesterol and blocked arteries instead of accepting the fact that I was different in more ways than just my physical appearance.

I looked to where my hands were resting against his chest, against his heart. I worded my next sentence carefully. "If what you say is true, why hasn't your heart frozen beneath my touch?"

"You don't consider me a threat."

"You *were* here to kill me. You've been ordered to. Technically, I might still consider you a threat."

He applied pressure with his palms to the small of my back and drew me in. I'd never felt such intense heat without being scalded, but this heat could only be good for me. I was certain of that, which was exactly why I wanted nothing more than to run away. If only I knew how to disapparate like Jareth did.

"I'm here to love you. Any threat you feel has nothing to do with the safety of your life, but the safety of your heart."

I shook my head vehemently and tried to push away while heated tears stung my frosty cheeks.

I knew it was a useless gesture, but I couldn't handle this intense exchange any longer. I'd spent all my life wishing for someone to love me. I would have settled for someone to simply *like* me, but the most emotion I'd ever managed to evoke was pained tolerance from women and a lusty, possessive need from men. Love, protection, consideration...even friendship were never part of the equation.

I'd come to the conclusion long ago that I was totally unlovable.

"I'm not a winter faerie, and I'm not your mate, and none of this is really happening." I choked on a sob and pounded his chest with my fists.

He captured my face with his hands and forced me to look him in the eye.

"Crysta, you are Fae. Why do you continue to deny the obvious?"

"Because it means I belong absolutely nowhere and with absolutely no one," I shouted, pushing him from me. "Do you think it's been easy to look like such a freak all of these years? Do you think it's been fun to be the only one capable of the things I am capable of? To be laughed at, made fun of, and bullied to the point where I literally woke up every morning wishing I was dead or at the very least someone else?" I scrubbed away the unwanted tears running unchecked down my cheeks. "I have fought so hard to be human, to be accepted, to find my place in this unfeeling world, and I've managed to discover moments of beauty, to carve out a special place for myself where no one can hurt me or belittle me ever again. I have to be human. I absolutely have to be what I've always believed myself to be. It's the only life I understand."

The pain in Jareth's eyes broke my heart a little because I knew it was for me, and I didn't want or need his pity.

He studied me for a few more moments before taking a tentative step forward. When I moved away from him his shoulders slumped in defeat.

"Whether you're human or Fae shouldn't matter to you at this point, Crysta. The simple fact that you're alive, that you're kind and decent, that you're strong and brave and funny and selfless...these are the things that make up the core of who you are. It's what drew me to you from the very beginning, even when I thought you were human. Our different races...well...they are just varied forms of existence. And if you need to believe that you're human in order to find your place in this world then I won't push the subject any further. Not tonight, anyway."

I sucked in a deep breath and let it out slowly.

"Thank you."

He nodded.

"You're welcome."

We stood facing one another for several seconds before I finally steadied my voice enough to speak again.

"I think it's been a very long day, and I need to get some sleep so I can—"

"Fill out those job applications tomorrow."

"Yes."

"May I go with you when you return them to their various owners?"

98

My eyes widened at this. I was grateful that Jareth understood my intense need to remain independent even though I struggled financially. I knew he had no intention of allowing me to pay my own rent, but I was grateful that he understood my driving compulsion to continue on as usual. To make my own way in this world.

"Yes. I'd like your company very much."

"Good. Then I wish you a good night, and I shall see you in the morning."

I nodded and turned to leave, but hesitated before heading down the hall to my room. Before I could talk myself out of it, I swiveled around and quickly moved toward him, throwing my arms around him and giving him a huge hug.

"Thank you."

His response was immediate and intense, pulling me close to his chest until I was flush against him and breathing in his scent of summer rain and freshly cut grass. He held me tightly before placing a soft kiss at my temple and then slowly released me.

"Good night, Crysta," he said in a hoarse whisper.

"Good night, Jareth."

Chapter Nine

After delivering about nine different job applications—
seriously, my feet were killing me—Jareth and I headed
back toward the apartment, each of us quiet and pensive,
no doubt due to the emotional conversation we had last
night.

The dynamic between us had changed a bit this
morning. Jareth seemed torn between needing constant
physical contact and giving me my own space. He tended
to reach for my hand and then immediately pull back. The
one time he did finally follow through and grab my hand,
his intense staring to gauge my reaction caused me to
avoid his gaze altogether. Within moments he had
released my hand, and I got the sinking feeling he thought
I was rejecting him.

It'd been like that all morning long, and I was starting to
hate the sadness that dampened his aura and energy.
After he'd taken another long, disheartened look my way,
I finally sighed and broke the oppressive silence between
us.

"Jareth, this may sound stupid, but I think we both
need a hug."

No sooner had I said it then his arms were completely

encircling me. He pulled me flush against him and buried his face in my neck.

"I'm so glad you said that. I understand your confusion concerning our relationship and your need for...uh... personal space, but not being allowed to touch you this morning has caused me more physical and emotional pain than I've ever experienced."

Wow.

Jareth's transparency when it came to his feelings was always such a surprise. No mind games with this one. And while I appreciated the honesty, I wasn't sure I liked the fact that my feelings mirrored his own.

"I never said we couldn't touch each other. In all honesty, I was struggling more with the idea that I'm Fae. As far as our relationship goes, I'm simply too scared to consider it."

He pulled back, sadness shrouding his features again.

"If you don't feel the same way, Crysta, I will understand, though I think it impossible due to the fact that we are fated mates."

I moved away, shaking my head and running both hands through my hair in frustration.

"Being in a relationship with you would be absolute heaven, Jareth, but the human realm is my world and I'm not leaving it. Your world is with the Fae, and one day you'll be their ruler." He opened his mouth to protest, but I hurried on. "You are going to leave me. Don't you see that? This attraction, this...whatever this is between us...it can't last."

"The very definition of a fated mate is an eternal one. With everything you've had to learn and understand about your inherent nature and heritage, this is one of the most important. I am yours, and you are mine. I am never leaving you."

"That's quite the declaration, but you'll forgive me if I don't believe that."

He looked bewildered by that statement. "You think I am lying?"

"No. I think you truly believe in fated mates and that there is a possibility that this...er...phenomenon between us signifies some destined love match, but we don't really know for sure, and this isn't Hollywood, okay? Love at first sight? That type of thing doesn't exist. It isn't plausible. It's a terrible long-term plan."

"Crysta, you make it sound as if feelings and affections are things that one can prepare themselves for. You were a complete surprise to me. A most welcome one, but not a situation I expected. I've been alive for over two hundred years and my experiences with women have been plentiful and varied, but overall, completely predictable. Yet you have surprised me at every turn."

"Whoa," I said holding up a hand. "I so did *not* need to hear about your plentiful relationships, thank you very much. And you're how old? Over two hundred? I'm not even eighteen yet. You can't be with someone who isn't legal!"

He shook his head dismissively. "Such a ridiculous custom to put an age limit on fertility. Once a woman is capable of bearing young, she should have every right to marry and begin a family if she so chooses."

I slapped my hand against my forehead. "Oh, my word. It's like you're incapable of recognizing what century this is. While that belief was popular a hundred years ago, these days most women tend to get an education before birthing children, which has nothing to do with why that law was created in the first place. No," I said, preventing him from voicing another opinion on the subject. "Forget it. I'm not diving down that particular rabbit hole with you." I started walking again, my emotions spiraling out of control.

He muttered something about my rabbit hole reference, but wisely chose to shut up afterward.

We were so different. This could never work. Hadn't every single conversation we had up to this point proved we were wrong for each other? I may have had feelings for this guy, but the more I learned about his past, who he was—his age, for heaven's sake—the more complicated everything became.

He caught up with me and grabbed my arm to stop me, turning me to face him.

"Crysta, this is not an issue I take lightly. A fated mate is rare and remarkably wonderful in its power to seal souls together. Once we perform the ceremony, you and I will always be one. I'm never leaving you. Why do you continue to doubt the possibilities? Why would you not believe in this? In us?"

I squeezed my eyes shut, wondering how to help him understand my fears on the subject.

"Do you love me, Jareth?"

"Yes."

My eyes popped open. I should have expected that honest and blunt statement, but it shocked the hell out of me.

"Based on what? My sparkling personality? The similarity in our life goals, hopes, and dreams? Do you even know what I want to major in?"

"Major in?" His scrunched up features relaxed. "Oh, you're referring to the educational systems at your ridiculous universities."

"I swear to you, if you add primitive to that description you will not be allowed into my apartment ever again."

He ran to catch up with me as I began hurriedly

moving on.

"If you are interested in majoring in something, then I am proud of you and support you in this endeavor, but anything you want to learn you can learn in the Fae realm. There is so much your people could teach you. Your education would never end."

"But do you even know what I want to study?"

"You're immortal. Eventually you'll study everything." He was so casual in the way he delivered that atomic bomb, I laughed out loud in response. It was either laugh or have one crazed panic attack.

His eyes narrowed as my laughter increased.

"Did I say something funny?"

I wiped my eyes with the tips of my fingers. "Yes, Jareth. You're saying I'm going to live forever, and personally I think that sucks. I've decided to actively reject immortality. I'd rather be human."

His look was comical. "You can't reject immortality any more than you can reject the fact that you are a faerie, Crysta."

"Watch me."

I was so majoring in dance, joining the San Diego Ballet Company, and eventually opening up my own dance studio, and there was no way I was going to let little things like the fact that I was possibly a faerie or immortal stop me. And I certainly wasn't going to let some pompous Fae prince talk me out of it.

"Crysta, you may be able to walk away from who you are and where you come from, but you can't walk away from me or what I feel for you."

"You *think* you're in love with me because you *think* I'm your fated mate," I threw over my shoulder. I wanted to be done with this conversation and get to my apartment as soon as possible so I could walk into my bedroom and slam the door behind me. With my luck, Jareth would probably just appear in my room.

"I *know* you are."

I snorted and shook my head. "People get bored of each other."

"Bored? What are you talking about?"

"They get sick of each other. They start fighting. They nit-pick and find things they hate about each other or they get interested in someone else and the commitment they made to one another begins to fade. I don't believe in fated mates or soul mates. I don't think you can sit there and tell me you're ready to commit to me and only me when we've known each other for three days. What happens when you finally realize that I'm not enough for you?"

He stopped me again and turned me around to face him. Then he reached for me, lifting my chin and bringing it closer to his tempting lips.

"I have always believed that a lifelong partnership can only be accomplished through fierce loyalty and a blind eye to the little idiosyncrasies each one of us possesses. I am fiercely loyal, Crysta. Of that, you will never have need to doubt."

Pretty words, but I wasn't about to give in and believe in this fated relationship he offered. It was too easy. Too perfect. It's not as if we were going to ride off into the sunset together and never look back. There were serious barriers to our potential relationship.

"And where will we live?"

He looked at me as if the answer was obvious.

"In my palace, of course."

"Ha! And I suppose you think I'll simply give up my life here and go learn how to be a faerie princess just because you think we're fated mates."

"What life? You live in a hell hole and you spend your days barely eking out a living."

I glared at him. Refusing to voice my hopes and dreams. Refusing to tell him about the dance academy I currently attended, the audition I had set for a few weeks from now, and how all of my rent money had gone to paying my tuition. He'd never understand it.

"And since I have nothing worth living for in this world, it only makes sense that I would jump at the chance to be the woman who stands by your side as you rule your kingdom for eternity."

"Well...yes," he said, though he was finally beginning to look a little uncertain. "Why wouldn't you? I can give you anything and everything you want. A stable place to live with a family who loves and cherishes you. Not to mention, I'll be giving you all of me."

He was so obtuse.

Generous?

Certainly.

Selfless?

In most cases, yes, but honestly what an idiot.

Everything was black and white with this guy, but learning I was a faerie hadn't changed my plans and it certainly hadn't changed my personality. It merely gave me an explanation as to why I'd always been such a freak of nature. I wasn't really human.

*Oh, mercy, I'm not even human.*

Time to visit that shrink.

"You weren't listening to me, Jareth. Would you be offering yourself to me if you didn't believe we were fated mates? If that fractured light that always appears between us had never shown itself would I even be alive today?"

I started walking again only to be stopped a bit more forcefully this time. I sighed and turned to face him.

"Yes," he stated.

"Why?"

"Because you didn't scream when I first appeared in your apartment, and when I told you I was there to kill you, you didn't even flinch. Those deep blue eyes of yours took me in with zero fear and an unhealthy amount of curiosity. If anything, you behaved as if you expected that something like this might happen. Like the idea of life and the opportunity to live it was simply too good to be true, and then you asked me to feed your cat once you were gone. It was by far the strangest reaction to death I'd ever encountered and it made me want to know you."

I had no idea what to say to that. I guess I *had* believed that it was all too good to be true. It was, after all, the day I'd found out about the audition, and it was also the day I'd found out that my roommate was planning on kicking me out of our apartment because she couldn't understand why I'd paid my tuition instead of paying my share of the rent.

I guess I'd just assumed that I could sleep in one of the bathrooms at the school if it came right down to it.

"I am not easily intrigued by anyone or anything, but your behavior drew me in and suddenly I couldn't get enough of you. I wanted to touch you, hear you speak, watch you move, understand your bizarre mode of speech, and protect your person at all cost. That first day with you was unlike any other, and I'm not too proud to admit that you taught me several important things that day and every day since."

I looked at him in wonder.

"You're over two hundred years old, Jareth. What could I have possibly taught you?"

"Compassion, forgiveness, and mercy."

I shook my head, barely understanding how I'd

managed to pull that off.

"Eddie," he said as if trying to jog my memory. "I was prepared to kill him for laying his filthy hands upon you. For threatening your life even though I had done the same thing not an hour earlier. You were merely a mark in the beginning, and within a short amount of time you'd become so precious to me that I was ready to strike down every male who dared touch you." He shook his head and rested his hand at my waist. "And what did you do when I stabbed him in the chest? You begged me to spare his life. To take him to a hospital. This man who had caused you so much grief and pain should have suffered for his crimes, but you chose mercy, and if you hadn't chosen that, I never would have realized that he was in thrall to your natural state. I would have killed an innocent man if not for your kind heart and tender feelings."

I lowered my eyes, unable to take in such a remarkable compliment. I really wasn't used to praise. I had no idea how to handle it.

"Fine. I impressed you with my decision, but that doesn't mean you love me."

"I may not know everything about you, but I don't need to know every detail of your life to determine if what I feel for you is permanent or fleeting."

I hated that I cared so much for this stupid, selfless, exasperating faerie, and that he'd managed to reduce me to tears even though I wanted to continue to argue and fight and possibly deny having similar feelings of my own that definitely leaned toward the more loving side of things. Jareth was decent, kind, loving, tender, compassionate, smart, and…and damn persistent. Didn't he know how much I wished he'd just give up already and leave me alone?

"Can we just go home, Jareth? Please?"

He wrapped me in his arms and allowed me to rest my head against his firm chest.

"Yes, sweet Crysta. I'll take you home now."

The compression was less nauseating this time, and I didn't lose my balance once the transition from pavement to carpet was complete. I slowly lifted my head from its resting place and looked up at him tentatively.

The concern in his face, and the soft tender look in his eyes made me realize that even though this relationship was most likely doomed to failure, and I was probably going to get my heart handed to me on a silver platter, experiencing love from Jareth on any level for any length of time would be better than never having experienced it at all. And I found myself believing that this particular man, this faerie prince would be worth every ounce of heartache I experienced once he finally realized he could do so much better.

"I still don't believe in fated mates, Jareth." I swallowed hard and forced the next words, the hardest words I'd ever spoken, from my mouth. "But I believe in you. If you say you love me, then I will believe it."

That admission alone nearly killed me, but my heart felt lighter only seconds later. The enormous grin on his face may have had something to do with that.

I'd been right. The force of his full smile nearly bowled me over. Geez. It was a good thing he was holding me upright.

"You'll never be sorry for believing in me. I'm not sure I deserve your trust, considering how we first met." We both chuckled at that. Definitely not the type of first date scenario you share with family and friends. "But as to whether or not we are fated for one another, well, there's only one way to find out."

"How?"

"We kiss."

I blinked in surprise and let out a soft chuckle.

"Coming from anyone else, I'd assume this was some line for hooking up."

"I have no idea what hooking up means," he muttered, glancing down at my lips and then back to my eyes.

"No, I suppose that term is pretty foreign to you." I smiled and he gave me an answering one in return. Then my frown faded for a moment.

"You're over-analyzing this, aren't you?"

I gave him a rueful smile, recognizing that he did, in fact, know me better than anyone else ever had.

"I just think that if a kiss is going to somehow prove that we're fated for one another then maybe we should avoid that for as long as possible."

"Why?" Worry clouded his voice and brought dark color to his eyes.

"Because I'd rather take that kind of pressure off us and just allow ourselves to be. Do we have to know for certain whether or not this is destiny if we already care about each other?"

He pondered my words for a moment and smiled.

"You want me to make sure I love you for you and not because I think you are my fated mate."

"Yes. That's what I want, and in the end, I think whatever we feel for one another, if it is right, will continue to grow on its own without the need to prove anything other than our feelings for one another."

He kissed my forehead and snuggled me under his chin.

"You are a wise woman. Yet another thing I love about you."

"There are so many things I love about you, Jareth. But your ability to compromise is definitely one of them.

Thank you for not pushing me on this."

"I think this course of action is wise, anyway. If I'm going to protect you, then I can't have the pull of our marks distracting me."

"Our marks?"

"If we are fated for one another then we each receive them after we've shared our first kiss."

"Oh," I swallowed uncomfortably and wished with all my heart that he hadn't told me that. How devastating would it be to not have the mark once we finally did kiss? Would that mean it was over? Would he simply leave me after that? I shook my head to dispel the doubts that already circled like vultures within my brain. I'd only been on board with this idea of a relationship for five minutes and already my insecurities were rearing their ugly heads.

No.

I told Jareth I would trust him and give him a chance. Give the idea of us a chance. Mark or no mark, we had to be the ones to decide if what we felt was, as he had so eloquently put it, fleeting or permanent, and no mark was going to make that decision for either one of us. In the end, I hoped the absence of a mark wouldn't matter, and that he would decide to love me either way.

Chapter Ten

Monday morning arrived like a freight train with its brakes out. I'd tossed and turned all night, feeling euphoric about my progressing relationship with Jareth one moment and then freaking out about the way he would most likely turn from me once my mark failed to show up. I even had a dream where Jareth kissed me, waited for my mark to appear, and when it didn't, shrugged his shoulders and disapparated from my life forever.

Needless to say, sleep had been an elusive dream.

The only thing that dragged me out of bed that morning was my nine o'clock class with my ballet instructor, Ms. Vivian, a Russian tyrant who had migrated over to the States thirty years ago to dance professionally. After twenty years of a highly successful career as a dancer and choreographer she decided to open up her own studio in the San Diego area. She was a strict, no-nonsense type of teacher, and I thoroughly enjoyed her despite the fact that she scared children and parents alike.

Now that I was preparing myself for this audition, she had added some private lessons to prep me. I wouldn't say I was her favorite. She really didn't play favorites, but early on in my training she had taken a special interest in me. She was probably harder on me and expected more from me than any other student at the moment, but that's how I liked it.

I wanted to be the absolute best when it came to technique, musicality, and gracefulness. I wanted to dance just like my idol Monique, and my plans of becoming a prima ballerina would not be jeopardized by my otherworldly heritage.

As I stumbled out of bed and stretched my arms high in the sky, Nala circled my legs and rubbed her midnight fur against my calf muscle. Naturally, the first person in the apartment entitled to breakfast was my short-haired feline, and don't think I didn't miss the fact that I considered her a person. She did too. I looked at my doorway, expecting Jareth to either be sitting there or making loud noises in the kitchen.

The apartment was silent. I might have assumed he decided to sleep in, but that seemed fairly out of character for him. He didn't like to sleep in Jami's room, and he was definitely an early riser. I checked my digital clock.

7:45.

My stomach knotted at the thought that maybe Jareth had had a change of heart in the middle of the night, and decided his feelings for me weren't as strong as he believed. I left my room and crossed the hall, peeking into Jami's room just in case Jareth had decided to sleep in her bed.

The room was dark and empty, the bed made, and the curtains drawn.

I walked down the hall and peered into the living room. No one.

The kitchen was equally devoid of life.

*Maybe he went to run a few errands?*

But I couldn't think of anything he might need to do or retrieve that he couldn't simply make apparate into existence. Why would he leave me? It was so unlike him? Wasn't I still in danger? Had he taken care of the threat to my safety and left me for another assignment?

Another female mark?

My insecurities were getting the better of me. This thought spiral had the potential to completely undermine my concentration. I had to focus if I wanted to survive my ballet class today.

I took a quick shower and then changed into my ballet leotard, tights, and leg warmers. I threw my toe shoes and ballet slippers in my dance bag with a bottle of water, some rosin, foam tape, toe pads, and a lightweight jacket. With my hair in a tight bun, my bag in my hand, and a bowl of fruit ready to go, I stood in the middle of my living room waiting for Jareth to magically appear out of nowhere just like he had the very first time I met him.

Nothing.

After twenty minutes of staring at the coffee table, willing his form into existence, I finally had to accept the fact that Jareth was gone.

And he was never coming back.

"Sorry I'm late," Jareth said behind me.

I jumped in surprise and whirled around. A mixture of irritation and relief fought for supremacy as I eyed his blue jeans and white T-shirt.

"Why are you dressed like that?" I asked.

He gave me a once-over and raised an eyebrow. "I could ask you the same thing. I don't remember you saying you had a ballet class today."

"Oh, well, I do, and I need to get going. I was ready to leave without you."

Jareth did not appear pleased with that response.

"Didn't Nuallan tell you I would be back by 8:30? I had to travel to the faerie realm and do some further investigating into your background. I couldn't allow anyone to know I had returned. That invisibility spell was not easy to use undetected. I also looked into the identity of your human parents and the accident they were in."

I blinked at the loaded information he shared. I wasn't sure what to address first, so I went with the easiest one.

"I haven't seen Nuallan all morning. Why did you feel the need to investigate my background? I could have told you the names of my parents and all the information I have about the car accident."

"Nuallan isn't here?" Jareth search the living room in agitation. "I don't understand. I left him here with explicit instructions to watch over you until I returned. This is not good."

"So you didn't leave me," I whispered before I could stop myself.

Jareth's eyes snapped to mine and narrowed.

"You awoke to no one in the apartment and thought I had abandoned you to whatever threat still hangs over your head," he stated. The pain in his eyes made me feel guilty and uncomfortable. He sighed. "Crysta, what must I do to convince you that I'm yours forever?"

He pulled me in for a comforting embrace and I eagerly accepted it. The turmoil and pain my previous thoughts had caused disappeared in the warmth of his touch.

"I know my feelings seem irrational to you, but my experiences haven't given me much cause for trust or confidence in relationships with others. I'm not accusing you of anything, but it will take some time for me to accept this opportunity for happiness. It just seems too good to be true."

His hand gently caressed the curve of my back, and I

relaxed even further in his arms.

"Well, I suppose I have all of eternity to convince you. To prove myself to you."

I looked up at him and smiled. "I suppose you do."

His eyes dropped to my lips and remained there for a moment. He inched himself closer until they were nearly touching mine. I knew it was probably best to avoid our first kiss until the threat to my safety was no longer an issue and Jareth and I could spend more time together, but at that particular moment, all of my logical reasons for avoiding the warm touch of his lips pressed against mine didn't seem nearly as significant as they had before.

Fortunately, Jareth's self-control was much stronger. He let his forehead rest against mine for a moment and then he released me with a groan.

"Once you finally allow me to kiss you, I probably won't stop for a very long time," he whispered.

A tingling sensation rippled along my spine. My lips quirked into a smile and I moved to the door before I gave in to the compulsion to throw caution to the wind.

"Promise?"

"The easiest promise I've ever made."

His heated look hinted at delivering the kind of kiss that set your nerve endings on fire.

"We'd better get going. Ms. Vivian will skewer me with her evil eye if I show up late to one of her classes."

"Your ballet teacher is a basilisk? How terribly unconventional."

"Slang, Jareth. Slang, although I'm seriously concerned that you just mentioned the word basilisk as if the creature actually exists."

"Of course, it does. Why else do you think J.K. Rowling had such intimate knowledge of the beast? Some authors are willing to do the most outlandish things for the sake of research."

I had to close my drooping jaw before I caught flies with it.

"Mind blown," I said. "I think we better stick to discussing what you discovered about my parents... among other things."

"We *could* just apparate to your dance studio."

"Allow me some semblance of normalcy, please. Even if it *is* just an illusion."

I walked out the door with Jareth's amused chuckle following close behind me.

Chapter Eleven

We hopped a city bus since I thought this type of normal, every day activity might be a good experience for the faerie prince. It wasn't too crowded, and Jareth began sharing with me what he had discovered.

According to him, everything seemed to look normal when it came to my birth date and hospital records, but my handsome assassin decided to do some digging and actually went to visit the nurse who helped deliver me seventeen years ago. How he managed to find her was beyond me, but the information he discovered was alarming.

"I found a charm embedded within her memory," he said.

"What? What do you mean you found a charm?"

"The nurse on duty that night was spelled to forget an incident that occurred a few hours after your alleged birth."

"Alleged? Pretty sure I was born, Jareth. There's really no way to debate that fact."

"But *when* you were born is what is up for debate here," he insisted. "The nurse on call said that you were born to Leslie and Carter Jensen at five-thirty-three in the evening, but the day you left home your measurements and weight resembled that of a baby who had been born two weeks before. She took note of the discrepancy as she took your measurements, but before she could record it, she was spelled to write something else in keeping with the weight and measurements of a newborn."

"Are you saying I was switched at birth or something? Someone deliberately gave me to Leslie and Carter and took their baby instead?"

"Not just someone, Crysta," Jareth said. He turned in his seat to look at me. "A faerie. Two faeries, to be precise."

"And how would you know that?"

"Every faerie leaves a specific signature with their biochemistry when casting a spell or charm. These two signatures were very distinct. Everyone in the Fae kingdom would recognize them and identify the two spell-casters if called upon to do so."

I stared at him and waited for the big reveal. When it wasn't forthcoming, I nudged him in the shoulder.

"So who are these well-known, totally recognizable faeries?"

Jareth appeared trouble. Almost spooked to say the names out loud and glanced around the bus to make sure we weren't being overheard.

Please. Like a conversation about faeries was even remotely remarkable on a public city bus in San Diego, California.

"Tuadhe d'Anu," he whispered under his breath.

"Come again?"

"The king and queen of the Unseely Court."

"I thought your father was the king."

"Of the Seely Court, yes, but there are two kingdoms within the Fae realm, and Insley and Rodri Tuadhe d'Anu were the ruling monarchs of the Unseely Court."

I didn't like where this conversation was headed.

"Were?"

He took a deep breath and let it out slowly before answering my question. "Crysta, they were murdered seventeen years ago along with their recently-born baby girl." He allowed that bombshell to sink in for a moment before he continued. "They must have known, somehow, that their lives and yours were in danger, and so they switched you with a human child to protect you in case the very worst happened."

My ears were ringing. I was certain I hadn't heard him right.

"Switched me. To protect me," I mumbled.

"Yes. You're a changeling, in a sense. Faerie children are substituted in a human family and the human children are taken as slaves."

I looked at him, appalled. "That's barbaric."

"That's tradition. In this instance, however, your parents pretended the human child was actually theirs, which means the threat to you was internal. It came from our own people, something I've suspected for quite some time."

"Why would you place faerie children with humans when you have such a low opinion of them?"

"It is mostly done to protect our children from threats on their lives. They grow up in a human family, but there is a faerie mentor to guide them throughout their adolescence so they can return to their people when they have matured."

"Well, I guess my faerie parents hadn't planned on my human parents getting into a car accident."

"It was no accident, Crysta."

"What?"

"As I stated before, a mentor is left to guide you as you come into your powers. They can be placed as a next door neighbor, teacher, governess, maid—"

"I get the point," I said. "So where was this mentor of mine, and why didn't he or she retrieve me when the car accident happened? Why didn't anyone claim me?"

Jareth nodded in approval. "You are asking all of the right questions, Crysta. Why indeed, unless they were in on the entire plot, and caused the accident themselves, leaving before they confirmed that everyone in the car accident had died. You were the sole survivor, were you not?"

All I could do was nod since I'd never been able to talk about it. I didn't remember it. What was there to say? I suppose I suffered from some form of survivor's guilt, but since I never really knew my parents, I could only mourn for who I imagined them to be. Not who they really were. Now come to find out these parents I'd longed to know for so long didn't really belong to me.

I belonged, instead, to the murdered king and queen of the Unseely Court. I was a winter faerie of royal blood.

Such a freak.

"So, they found out about the switch after they killed my par...the king and queen, and quickly tried to rectify the situation by murdering my human parents and me in the process."

"Yes," Jareth nodded gravely. "The king and queen were betrayed by someone they trusted. Someone who knew what they had done."

"Clearly, someone wanted the throne, or the power, or whatever...so my parents and I were murdered to get it. A relative, maybe?"

Jareth shook his head. "The motive behind all of this isn't nearly so obvious. The order for your assassination came from the Seely Court. Not the Unseely Court. Even if there was a winter faerie who wanted you dead, there were no other legitimate heirs, and Roderick, the late king's brother, your uncle, lived his life as a hermit before being pressed into servitude for the court. Believe me when I say, your uncle wanted nothing to do with the throne and yet it fell to him either way. He'll be relieved to discover you survived, once we finally unearth the masterminds behind this traitorous plot."

"Well, I hope he doesn't assume I'll be happy to take over or anything. I definitely have plans for the future, but they don't include ruling the Unseely Court."

Jareth's face darkened and he opened his mouth to say something, but our stop arrived just in time.

"This is us," I said in a cheery tone. I jumped off that bus before he decided to try and convince me that my destiny involved the Fae realm, an impromptu wedding, and an icy crown.

\*\*\*

Ms. Vivian was already in full battle mode the minute we walked into the studio, meaning, she was already yelling at the piano player to play the piece at the exact tempo she wished. Her eyes focused on me with hawk-like precision. I swear I sometimes felt like a small rat whenever her gaze zeroed in. She missed absolutely nothing, which was why I adored her so much. Flawless technique was something she nit-picked to death, but I wouldn't have it any other way. The moment her eyes alighted on Jareth a startling transformation took place. Her lips actually turned up at the corners in a hint of a smile, softening the severe lines of her face due in large part to the stiff bun she always wore to control her silver hair.

"Ah, Crystiana," she said as she glided forward with the grace of a gazelle. She gave me a few air kisses and then stepped back to study Jareth with unveiled curiosity. He stiffened in amazement at my side.

"I don't know how you knew we would need a leading male for today, but I do believe this young man shall do quite nicely."

I gave her a blank stare. "Do what nicely?"

"Be your partner for rehearsal, of course. Did you assume I would have him running to fetch us an overpriced cappuccino? Don't be ridiculous."

"My partner? I wasn't aware that prepping for auditions involved partner dancing."

She tsked at me in disapproval.

"There will be two dances you must learn for your audition. A solo piece, more specifically the *Sugar Plum Fairy* and a *pas de deux* from *Giselle* act two."

"But Ms. Vivian, my friend doesn't know how to dance."

"No?" She quirked a sardonic brow in his direction. "He did the last time I saw him. I believe you put on an impressive performance at the summer festival. How long ago, Jareth?"

I looked between the two of them in amazement.

"You two know each other?" I asked.

Jareth shook his head in wonder. "That particular performance you refer to happened over fifty years ago."

"I assume you still remember the choreography," she said.

"Does a faerie ever forget, Ms. Vivian?" he asked.

She smiled in delight. "No, my prince, we most certainly do not." Then she turned to me. "I always suspected you were Fae, but I had no idea you knew our prince."

"I've known him less than a week," I said in a strained voice.

My thoughts zipped around my head in an attempt to make sense of this new development. My ballet teacher and Jareth knew each other. She was a faerie, and clearly much older than she appeared.

Jareth danced? Ballet?

Ms. Vivian's eyes glittered with interest. "I take it you were not aware of your heritage until recently?" She looked at Jareth. "And why is the Seely Court interested in a changeling? I assume you are here at their behest?"

I shook my head to dispel the crazy descending, and blurted out a curt summary. "He was sent to assassinate me and decided not to since our skin lights up whenever we touch each other."

Her eyes shot to Jareth's, worry creating sharp creases between her brow.

"You protect her now?"

"Yes," he said in determination.

"You understand the sacrifice you must be willing to make for your fated mate, Jareth? Her home is in this realm."

His jaw strained with tension. Clearly he didn't like what she alluded to, and I was busy trying to keep track of this verbal ping pong between them. Hell. I still had trouble getting used to the idea that these two knew each other.

"That decision is yet to be determined," he stated stiffly.

She gave him an agitated glare.

"You cannot ruin everything she has worked so hard for."

"She deserves more than this life she leads."

"Oh, the Fae and their superiority complex." Ms.

Vivian pointed a finger at his chest. I watched in amazement as Jareth took an uncertain step back. Even *he* was intimidated by her. "You'll allow her to choose or you will lose her forever. Be very careful, Prince of the Seely Court. The Universe does not revolve around your very black and white ideals." She squared her shoulders and took in a deep breath. Tranquility descended around her like a sudden mist of magic. "And now, we work. Crystiana?"

I nodded and set my bag down, deciding I didn't want to delve too deeply into that obviously loaded conversation. I put my ballet slippers on and went through my exercises at the barre starting with *plié, tendu,* and moving on to more complicated exercises such as *frappé* and *grand battement*. I didn't realize that Jareth had joined me at the barre until finishing the first exercise on one side and turning to repeat it on the other. He gave me a grin at my look of shock, and then I had to fight to stay focused every time I was faced with Jareth's backside as he also performed the barre exercises in sweats he hadn't been wearing on the way over. No doubt he just had them apparate on his person like it was nothing.

After several more exercises we moved on to center-work in the middle of the floor. *Ports de bras* were followed by an *adagio*, which were slow combinations of movements and *pirouettes* or turns and large and small jumps. *Petit* and *grand allegro* combinations. I kept my eyes on the mirror before me and tried not to allow Jareth's impressive technique and handsome blue eyes to distract me from my own work. After forty-five minutes, Ms. Vivian was ready to have us work on the *pas de deux* from Giselle.

"I assume you are still familiar with the choreography, Jareth," Ms. Vivian said.

"If you are still using the variation from Marius Petipa then I think I should be able to follow along."

I stared at him in wonder. Seriously? The fact that he'd ever danced *Giselle* in the first place made him even more attractive than before, but he still remembered it? Who knew how long ago that had happened. I didn't even want to think about the girl he'd partnered with.

"Well, let's turn the music on and see what kind of a disaster I'll be working with."

Now I had danced as the principal in *Giselle* two times in the last two years, so choreography wasn't an issue for me, but the idea that we should simply begin dancing without ever having gone over the choreography or partnering together seemed ludicrous to me. We didn't understand each other's styles and movements yet. We weren't comfortable with each other in that respect. I would have felt much more at ease if she had insisted we mark it first.

"You never told me you could dance," I hissed.

He gave me an infuriating grin.

"You never asked, Crysta."

As the beautiful music began, I took up position and flayed him with a nervous glance.

Disaster, indeed.

*Giselle* is a story of a young peasant girl who falls in love with Albrecht, a royal disguised as a commoner. She isn't aware that he is betrothed to someone else and they dance together at a festival, falling in love. She eventually realizes that the man she loves is betrothed to someone else and her weakened heart is unable to handle the sorrowful dance she performs. She dies in his arms. In act two, Albrecht goes to visit her grave deep in the forest and is ensnared by ethereal wilis, spirits of women who have been jilted and exact revenge on any man crossing their path by forcing them to dance to their death. Giselle has become one of them, but pleads that they spare him.

In this dance, he asks for her forgiveness and she freely gives it to him. Even though it is a dance that both Albrecht and Giselle dance together, Giselle begins it alone in the center of the stage.

The soft strains of a solo viola began, and I immediately responded to the music, the mood, the intent with which the steps required. I lifted my leg in *développé* and turned to *arabesque*, which was made difficult due to the required slowness of the movements, and then I fully immersed myself within the dance.

*I am intervening on Albrecht's behalf, and my love for him, my desperation that he be saved must translate into every muscle, every movement, every facial feature as I slowly dance across the floor. As Giselle, I am stuck in my position, in limbo between an unmarked grave because of my suicide, but I don't belong with the Wilis since I have refused to hurt Albreicht.*

*I belong nowhere, and find my limbs and movements restricted to one spot. Then Albrecht joins me. He supports me through sorrowful lifts and turns, filled with remorse at the fate of the peasant girl he cast aside. The adagio is solemn and mournful, passionate and pleading. In the end, I grant him forgiveness and my love saves him from the Wilis.*

At the first touch of Jareth's hand at my waist, I felt the room slip away, envisioning an enchanted forest filled with wraith-like spirits intent on hurting the man I loved. Someone I could never have. Someone who would never be mine. Bringing my right leg into *développé* and brushing my left foot up against my right, I reached out in arabesque with my leg pointed back as Jareth gently lifted me high above his head and slowly lowered me to the ground where I gracefully reached my arms forward and stayed on point as he turned me slowly in a circle. I then returned to first position and jumped slightly as he lifted me high. I arched my back, looking as if I did a leap in a circle with his supportive hands placed at my waist.

We continued our movements as if we had danced them together a million times over. Connecting and contracting in perfect symmetry. Our lines, our steps, and the energy with which we danced matched and then grew together with the same intensity. With Jareth's support, I honestly believed I had a chance at achieving everything I'd ever dreamed of. As the dance came to a close and the music faded into silence, I drew in a tentative breath and held it for a moment. I just wanted to savor what I knew to be one of the most profound moments of my life. The moment when I acknowledged to myself just how much I wanted and needed Jareth in my life, and how beautiful a partnership with him would be.

"I think," Ms. Vivian said, "we do it again. Yes?"

"Yes," Jareth said in a whisper. "Let's do it again."

From the look in his eye it was clear I had exceeded any expectations he may have had in regards to my dancing. Feeling gratified at his reaction, I simply nodded and we started the *pas de deux* from the beginning.

Chapter Twelve

Jareth remained disturbingly quiet after rehearsal, and I didn't dare engage him in any meaningless chit chat after what we had just shared together. I was certain he was mulling a few things over concerning his future and mine.

*"You'll allow her to choose or you will lose her forever."*

Ms. Vivian's warning to him rang through my head, reminding me that a relationship between the two of us was at the very least complicated and at the very most completely impossible.

Choose what? Choose him? I would choose Jareth a thousand times over, but at what cost? What exactly would I be giving up? This world that I knew and loved? My dreams of becoming a professional ballerina? Just what was I willing to give up in order to be with Jareth?

Everything, I realized. For some reason, dancing with him had crystallized that knowledge into one irrefutable truth.

Everything.

I could dance professionally for the rest of my life, but without Jareth, every moment would be meaningless.

I couldn't begin to express how much that realization pissed me off. Suddenly furious at him for disrupting my life, weaseling his way into my heart, and then giving me no other choice but to love him above everything else that was important to me, I stopped walking long enough to turn and punch him as hard as I could in the arm.

He stepped back in utter shock and raised his hands to fend off another attack.

"Crysta, what in the world is the matter with you?"

"You," I growled as I ducked under a defensive arm and nailed him in the stomach. The whoosh of air he let out was extremely satisfying. Since I couldn't disappear into thin air like he could, I leveled him with one more thwack to the solar plexus and stormed off.

"Crysta," he called after me, running to catch up, hardly even affected by my attack.

"You couldn't just show up, do your job, and end me, could you?" I muttered. "Oh, no. You just had to satisfy your curiosity. Get to the bottom of our glowing skin, my crazy hair, and my actual parentage." He grabbed my arm, but I shoved him off and kept power walking away. "You are wholly to blame for all of this, do you understand me?"

He grabbed my arm and spun me around, forcing me to face him.

"All of what?" he asked, clearly exasperated.

"This entire ordeal. This idea that I don't belong here, in this world with these humans. The idea that I belong with you wherever you live and wherever you have a life and responsibilities. You've made me care about you and depend on you to the point that I feel as if I may stop breathing if I never see you again, but it's not like we can have a long distance relationship between realms while you rule the faeries and I go on to professionally dance like one." I stopped and ran my hand through my hair, tearing up and cursing myself for it. "I won't give it up,

Jareth. I don't want to let go of everything I've worked so hard for, but the thought of losing you makes me want to lie down and never dance again."

He gently lifted my chin and brushed a few stray tears from my cheeks. His kind eyes took in my distraught face and his concern for me deepened the faint lines surrounding his mouth and eyes.

"Do you love me, Crysta?" he asked.

"Yes." I let out a ragged sob.

He crushed me to him in a warm embrace and used his magic to take us back to our apartment. When I brought my watery eyes to his, and saw the lock of his jaw and felt the intensity of his determination, I knew exactly what was coming.

My breath hitched as he pulled me closer and crushed his lips to my own, searing me with the most intense heat I'd ever experienced. I felt as if fire had consumed the whole of us, but never for one moment was I afraid of being burned. His lips explored the tender corners of my mouth and then gently massaged my bottom lip as I held tightly to him and matched his wonderful kisses with my own. I wasn't afraid of Jareth, and I wasn't afraid to love him, but I was desperately afraid to lose him. After a few more moments of intense kissing, we came up for air.

"Crysta? Does this mean you'll come back home with me someday?" He lifted my chin with the curve of his finger and forced me to look him in the eye. His own eyes held questions, and I didn't know what answers to give him. Then his eyes flicked upward and a huge smile spread across his lips.

His full smile made my knees go numb.

"What is it?"

"Proof. The kind of proof I was hoping might give you a little more faith in our future together. Proof that you and I are meant for one another, though I would have fought for you until my last breath whether this outcome had occurred or not."

I gave him a questioning look.

"What proof are you talking about? Proof of what?"

"That we are fated for one another. You have a permanent mark on the right side of your temple now." He leaned forward and softly kissed the mark.

I stepped away from his embrace and ran to the small mirror hanging above the desk against the wall. I stared long and hard at myself, not recognizing the young girl reflected before me. I hadn't just received a strange mark on the side of my face—my whole being had transformed. My hair was the blinding white color I had worked so hard to cover, and my eyes appeared more slanted and frosty blue than ever before. I pulled my white hair behind my ears and stopped short. Gone were the surgically rounded tips I'd spent so much time saving for. They'd reverted back to their original pointy ends.

I might have felt frustrated that all my hard work in the pursuit of blending in was now a non-issue, but my strange "birth defects" no longer looked ugly or undesirable. I felt beautiful for the first time in my life.

I studied the mark on my temple. Two eternity symbols layered in gold overlapped and intersected with one another. The mark tingled slightly at my touch. I saw Jareth come up behind me and place his hands on my shoulders. The tenderness of his touch, the way his eyes sought mine and gave me a hopeful, almost pleading look made my legs go rubbery.

"Crysta, please say you'll stay with me in the faerie realm once it is safe for you to do so."

I studied the mark on my temple, my pointed ears and white hair, and realized that Jareth had accepted all of me.

The before and after versions of me. I didn't have to hide, change, or defend who I was, and I didn't have to be ashamed of what I used to be.

"I'll stay with you, Jareth," I said.

He spun me around and pulled me to him, finding my lips with his and kissing me senseless. I nearly jumped out of my skin when a loud banging noise sounded to my left. Nuallan had apparated right next to us and plowed into the coffee table. I jumped in surprise and then narrowed my eyes into a killer glare.

"Nuallan, I need you to get on board with the concept of knocking," I said.

"We don't have time for that," he replied. Then he really took me in and his harried look only intensified.

"It's true. She's your fated mate and one of the royals we thought murdered," he rubbed his hands over his face. "This is very bad, Jareth."

"What's wrong?" Jareth asked.

"Your father knows I lied. He knows Crysta was never dealt with and that you never moved on to a new assignment. I don't know how he found out, but he is definitely coming here." He pointed to me. "Her life will be over when he does."

There was heavy silence, punctuated by Jareth's angered breathing.

"Nuallan, what exactly are you getting at?"

"Perhaps I can answer such a troubling question," said a deep voice from behind us.

Jareth and I both turned to look at the door, where a slightly older version of Jareth stood. My faerie assassin came to attention in the presence of this rather imposing figure.

"Father?"

The older faerie gave him a somber nod. "Jareth, I

became alarmed when you did not return to our realm within the time specified, but when Nuallan assured me you were simply eager to take on more and prove yourself," he paused to give Nuallan a death glare, "I decided to allow you some space. Imagine my concern when I discovered your original target. Due to an unfortunate oversight amongst my leaders, you were given the task to kill someone you were never meant to have any contact with." He paused to turn his hate-filled glare on me. "Ever. You were not meant to be here." There was real fire in this old faerie's eyes. I took a slight step backward as Jareth positioned himself in front of me.

"I demanded the assignment due to the nature of the target. I had no idea I was being sent to kill my future bride, and up until a few moments ago, I had no idea you were the one who ordered her death."

The king laughed in derision. "We took great pains to exterminate all of the Tuadhe d'Anu family for this very reason. Our seer became aware of the eventual union when the princess was born, but uniting faeries from two different courts would have created a magical imbalance within the kingdom. Both of you cannot be king and queen over the Seely and Unseely Courts. They must remain separate and distinct."

Jareth's look of displeasure intensified. I was happy to not be on the receiving end of his righteous wrath. His comment to his father came out controlled, almost polite.

"It was quite sloppy of you, letting her get away."

The king flicked his hand in annoyance.

"You will hand her over to me and leave the human realm immediately."

Jareth shook his head. "If we are fated for one another then the outcome of our union will not end in chaos. You'll not consider giving this union a chance? It is clearly fated.

The marks are not something that can be faked. There must be a reason for this."

"The only way for that to occur is for you to give up your birthright to the throne, step down, and allow your younger brother to take your place. But that would mean giving up everything. It would mean ruling the Unseely Court. And neither you nor this changeling know anything about the Unseely Court. Are you willing to give up everything you've worked so hard for, for this faerie?"

Jareth's silence tore at my heart a little. I raised my eyes to his, but couldn't get a handle on his thoughts, his face was void of emotion. I understood the choice he faced now, and I honestly didn't expect him to pick me. That's why his next words surprised me.

"Yes, I'm willing to give up my birthright"

His father sputtered in disbelief. "I can't let you do that. I did everything I could to make certain you would never feel compelled to make such a destructive decision."

"Father, I do not have to be king of the Seely Court to be happy, and Rolin is more than capable of ruling in my stead."

His father shook his head no.

"You said I had to be willing to give it all up, and I am. Perhaps that is part of the future the seer envisioned. Perhaps this is best."

"I am king, and I know what is best. We're not allowing the direction and fate of the Seely Court to be determined by a princess from the Unseely Court. Their only thought is for murder and conquest. They want to destroy us all."

Jareth rolled his eyes as if this subject had been brought up between them repeatedly and was one they never agreed upon.

"Paranoia, Father. You turned into everything you fear

when you ordered Crysta's assassination."

"I won't allow it."

"We've already exchanged our marks. Half the ceremony has been completed. This cannot be reversed."

"It can if she's dead."

Jareth's eyes narrowed and his nostrils flared as he gritted his teeth. He took in a deep breath and let it out slowly, though I sensed his temper reaching a breaking point.

"You are discussing the murder of the woman I love. Do you honestly think I'll just stand by and let you kill her? Any of you?" He directed that last shot at Nuallan, who stared wide-eyed and open-mouthed.

I'd almost forgotten he was there.

"I didn't murder an entire faerie bloodline only to be thwarted by a silly Fae tradition," his father continued.

"Fated mates have nothing to do with tradition."

"You cannot abdicate the throne, and she cannot live so long as you have feelings for her."

Jareth stared at his father for a few moments and then looked at me, communicating something so profound and deep, I failed to grasp it until it was too late.

"Then I'm afraid you have given me no choice, Father." Jareth stood taller, withdrew his dagger from its sheath at his waist, and began tracing a small, thin cut across the length of his right palm. "By the gods of our forefathers and the first faeries of our realm—"

"Jareth, you will stop this at once," the king thundered, but his son paid him little heed. The king began to move toward us, but Jareth murmured some incantation and threw his left hand up, blocking his father's advance. "Consider the consequences!"

"We must do this quickly." Jareth turned to me. "I denounce my birthright and position in the Seely Court of faeries, and seal my life, my soul, and my essence with this winter faerie, Princess Crystiana Tuadhe d'Anu, and by so doing, relinquish any and all claims to the rule and reign of the Seely Court forever." He quickly slashed the palm of my hand, making me squeal in surprise. Then he placed his bleeding one in mine. "Crysta, repeat after me."

I stared at the blood seeping from the sides of our joined palms. Too stunned to protest, I repeated the words he gave me. "I seal my life, my soul, and my essence with this summer faerie, Prince Jareth Tuatha d'Dannan."

Jareth ignored the ravings of his father. He only had eyes for me. "This union is now permanent and can never be undone." White light exploded between us and then enveloped us completely. I felt a strange tingle encompass the whole of me. Not just my physical being, but my soul felt as if it was shedding its outer layer and becoming one with something better, something greater than myself.

When the light finally dimmed and my eyes adjusted to the change, Jareth and I still stood in the middle of my living room with a sputtering Nuallan and an enraged Fae monarch.

In a gravelly voice the king said, "The repercussions of these actions will effect an entire kingdom."

Jareth inhaled a fortifying breath and gave his father a cold look. "Just your kingdom, Father. Just yours."

"I will find a way to undo what you've done, my son." His murderous eyes captured mine. Their pupils contracted and thinned into a dark line. I shivered at the malevolence they radiated. "And when I do, this insignificant faerie will most certainly die."

His frame flickered before us and then vanished out of sight. I stared at the space the king vacated and wondered if I would ever feel safe in this apartment again.

"How could you do this, Jareth? Why would you do

this?" Nuallan said in a grave voice.

"What did you do?" I asked.

"You mean besides giving up his right to the throne?" Nuallan shouted. "Jareth, are you insane?"

I shook my head in disbelief.

"Jareth, you gave up a kingdom for me."

He shrugged his shoulders as if his selfless sacrifice on my behalf hadn't been enormous. "I'd give up much more to keep you safe."

"Why?"

"I love you, Crysta. Haven't you figured that out yet?"

I blinked several tears and buried my face against his chest.

"I think I'm starting to."

"While this is all very moving, it still doesn't solve anything. That damned spell you just cast complicates things considerably," Nuallan continued.

I raised my eyes to Jareth's. "What spell? What exactly did you do?"

Jareth appeared agitated as if I might not like his answer.

"I tied my soul to yours."

"You did more than that," Nuallan said. He turned to me, worry creasing his brow. "Your souls are linked now."

"What, like a marriage?" I asked in disbelief.

"It goes beyond marriage, Crysta," Jareth said. "Because faeries live forever, it is sometimes unbearable for one spouse to continue on for eternity without the other. Though we are immortal, there are still ways we can be killed. In some situations couples will bind their souls together so that if one faerie dies, then the other soon follows."

I gaped at him in disbelief. "You outmaneuvered your

father. If he succeeds in killing me, he kills you too. You've put your life in danger for my sake."

Jareth took my hand in his and brought it to his lips. "While it's nice to pretend that what I did was brave and selfless, in reality, I know my father will never make another attempt on your life while I'm linked to you. I haven't risked my life anymore than I usually do, Crysta, but I *have* managed to ensure that no one will endanger yours ever again."

"And if your father makes good on his threat to undo the spell linking the two of you, what then?"

Jareth leveled a harsh look at Nuallan.

"It is impossible to reverse this."

"Impossible once the two of you are married. Without the marriage ceremony strengthening the link, there is a way to undo it."

Jareth shook his head in denial, but I wanted to know exactly what the risks were for both of us.

"How can it be undone?" I asked.

Nuallan shuddered. "One of you must renounce your commitment to the other, deny your love, and...and..."

"...willingly perform a counter-spell that severs the link, cutting our souls in two," Jareth finished. "It's incredibly painful."

I looked between the two of them, waiting for a far more treacherous answer. When none was forthcoming, I gave Jareth a reassuring smile.

"That means the ball's in our court." I stated.

"Jareth, do translate," Nuallan said.

I impatiently continued. "If the spell can only be reversed by one of us then it will never happen. I have no intention of ever denying my love for you."

Jareth's somber look lightened considerably, but his eyes were still tinged with a heavy sadness.

"Unfortunately, Crysta, it may be possible for my father to find a way to compel or coerce you into severing the link. One simple mind control spell would force you to do anything the spell-caster wished."

"You have to marry her as soon as possible," Nuallan said. "It's the only way to tie up that weakness and make Crysta yours forever."

I tensed at this. Marriage was a huge step for anyone, and I was only seventeen years old. I understood that this move might be the safest play in order to keep me safe, but did we really want to be forced into making such a huge commitment to one another to keep his father from killing me? Marrying for protection and safety didn't sit well with me. I wasn't human, I happened to be the current heir of the Unseely Court, I loved Jareth and he loved me, and now our souls were linked together.

If I died, he died.

It was too much.

Jareth placed his hands on my stiff shoulders and massaged them with his nimble fingers.

"For the record, I already want to marry you, so don't go over-analyzing things by assuming my father has forced my hand."

Dang. He knew me so well.

"Why can't you be coerced into performing a counter-spell?" I asked.

Nuallan and Jareth both laughed at my question. I thought the reaction was a little inappropriate, considering the severity of the situation.

"Jareth is a powerful faerie with full command of his magic," Nuallan said with a hint of pride. "There isn't a faerie in the world capable of forcing him to do anything he would not wish."

I nodded, understanding settling heavy in my gut.

"So I'm the weak link here."

Jareth wrapped me in his arms and pulled me to him.

"I don't want you to worry about this anymore. Do you understand me? You aren't ready for marriage, and we've got an audition coming up that we need to prepare for."

"Just like that? We're not going to consider the danger you are in because of me? We're not going to talk about the fact that you gave up an entire kingdom for me or what the repercussions are for you now?" I waited for him to communicate with me, but he glued his lips together in a taut, thin line. I turned to Nuallan. "Can he ever go back to the faerie realm?"

Nuallan looked at his prince, probably wondering if he dared risk giving me an answer, but my glare must have been a bit more motivating.

"He can return, Crysta, but why would he? He has nothing to return home to, and he cannot leave you weak and defenseless in this realm."

Jareth's sacrifice came into focus at that moment. He hadn't just given up his kingdom. He'd given up his life, his friends, his family, his world, everything to ensure that I remained safe. He hadn't planned on his father being the threat we fought against. He hadn't planned on falling in love with me and then turning his back on everything else.

But he'd done it.

He'd done it for me.

"Nuallan, if I learned how to wield my magic would that protect me from another faerie's compulsion?"

Nuallan studied me with a curious glint in his eye.

"Yes, of course, but the best way to do that is within the Fae realm. The magic there is more heightened. You would have greater access to your powers and more control as you learned to use them."

"Crysta what are you thinking?" Jareth asked.

"You said my uncle would be very happy to learn that I am alive. You said he never wanted to rule the Unseely Court in the first place."

"Yes?"

Jareth's monumental sacrifice on my behalf solidified my decision. He had given up everything to protect me, and I was more than willing to do the same for him.

"I hear there's a position open in the Unseely Court. You wouldn't be interested in ruling a kingdom with me, would you?"

Shock slackened the muscles in his jaw. His blue eyes widened in disbelief.

"You would do that? Give up your life here for me?"

"You're my life, Jareth. And since we'll both be living forever, I'm sure I'll get another crack at professionally dancing in a century or two." I held my hand out to him as an offering. "Are you gonna help me make things right? It seems to me the faeries might benefit from a king and queen who aren't totally unhinged."

Jareth took my hand and placed a gentle kiss upon my cheek. Then he took me in his arms and kissed me absolutely senseless before letting me come up for air.

"It would be my honor and privilege, sweet Crysta."

I rested my head against his chest and reveled in the love and security I felt within his arms.

"Well, now that we've got that settled, there is one thing I want to make very clear before we leave," I said.

"What's that?"

"Under no circumstances will I ever refer to you as, Your Majesty."

Jareth let out a soft chuckle and nestled my head just under his chin.

"You wouldn't be my sweet Crysta if you did."

Don't Forget

Thank you so much for downloading *My Fair Assassin*. I hope you enjoyed the first book in the *Paranormal Misfits Series*. The second book in the series, Runaway Heiress, will release in the spring of 2017. It stinks to have to wait for more books to read, which is why I hope you took advantage of my offer to grab yourself another free book. Here it is in case you haven't grabbed it yet. Just click on this link here.

# Be Part Of The

For

Pic

"Young Adu
*Instruments*
this series.

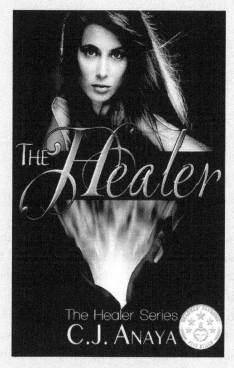

## Author's Note

Thank you for reading My Fair Assassin. I hope you enjoyed this novella. This was first published in a fun paranormal anthology called *Strange and Lovely*. I encourage you to check that book out in order to discover other talented authors of paranormal romance.

I originally wrote this for my niece who was struggling with her own self-esteem and self-worth. I wanted her to understand that the differences in her facial features were beautiful, distinct, and unique.

It's hard to find yourself in high school. It's hard to appreciate the differences you bring to the equation when every high school "hierarchy" has its own code of what is acceptable and what isn't. Being proud of who you are can be a challenge when faced with mean girls and all of their drama.

I wanted my niece and any other girls struggling with their appearance to understand that the right man, the right friends, the right people will always love and accept you for who you are and what you bring to the table. To be caught up in changing any of what makes you beautiful for the approval of others will only make you unhappy in the end.

As Jareth so aptly questioned, "You removed your most beautiful, defining features so humans would love you?"

It's hard to tell that to a teenager or even an adult without getting an eye-roll or two, so maybe wrapping this lesson in a paranormal package will catch their attention and drive home this important message.

Other Books By C.J. Anaya

**The Healer Series**

The Healer: Book 1
*The Black Blossom: Book 2*
*The Grass Cutter Sword: Book 3*

***

*Double Booked*
*Marry Your Billionaire*

About The Author

I began writing short stories for family and friends
when I was thirteen years old. My vivid imagination and
love of mysteries and romances eventually led me to

following my own dreams of becoming a published author. I also do some book review work for SDE Magazine on the side.

I'm a huge fan of The Mindy Project, Hugh Jackman, and binge eating any and all things chocolate.

Who isn't?

As a mother of four awesome kids I'm usually playing beauty salon with my daughters—my four-year-old shaved my arm one time while I was helping another daughter with her homework. Yep. That happened— getting my fanny kicked in Mario Kart by my snarky little son, and making out with my deliciously handsome Latin lover, aka, my hubby.

Stop by and say hello to C.J. Anaya on her website at http://authorcjanaya.com

Facebook: https://www.facebook.com/cjanayaauthor

Twitter: CJAnaya21

Made in the USA
Columbia, SC
12 December 2017